My Cookie

A DIRTY BOSS ROMANCE
BOOK TWO

C.M. STEELE

THE STEELE PRESS

Julien & Marilyn

Julien: After going through numerous candidates, I've found the best baker to work alongside me. Marilyn Shaw's baked goods are works of art that rival my own. She bakes the most delicious desserts, but I don't want them. I want her.

Marilyn: I could have my own bakery if I wanted, and my older brother would have it set up for me in a heartbeat. The problem is that I have something to prove. I'm not a spoiled girl who gets everything her brother throws her way, but people have always assumed it, so I've worked tirelessly to get perfect grades in my pastry program. Now, to show off my skills in a bakery. The only problem is everyone believes I got the job by sleeping with my new boss. And I am…

CHAPTER
One

MARILYN

I've just checked into my hotel room in downtown Chicago when my besties text me that they're on their way here and only a few minutes out.

"Yay," I squeal. Technically, there's no reason for me to rent a hotel room for the night when I live nearby, but my brother wanted to spoil me rotten with all the amenities before my big day tomorrow. Besides, they have a very nice bar downstairs for us to party in without needing to alert my brother's guards, who are extremely good at their job.

Lacey and Casey are out to cause trouble tonight, so we all promised to wear something super sexy and well, I'm just a very good friend. I found this faux leather outfit, and I'm obsessed how it fits my figure perfectly. It's not a dress I'd ever wear outside, but for them, I'll do it. I'm just hoping my brother's guards don't rat me out or that he's too blissfully happy with his wife to be bothered with my life tonight.

Scurrying my bum down to the lobby, I spot two guys heading into the bar and I nearly trip because I come to a complete stop and admire the tall one's profile which immediately grabs my attention. Every feature on his face fits perfectly, like it's been chiseled out of the finest marble from the greatest sculptor. Lips that beg to be kissed, even with that perfected scowl forming.

I wish he'd turn all the way so I could see all of him. My body bursts to life with desire for the first time, and I crave more. Damn, I need a drink now.

"Mare," Lacey shouts, causing my tall distraction's scowl to deepen even though he refused to look in the direction of the noise.

I spin around to the revolving doors and see my besties coming in, looking hot in their outfits. We're all wearing little black dresses, but I'm the only one in black heels. The girls both have matching black dress sandals.

"Case, Lace, I'm so glad you're here." I throw my arms around them, and we squeeze tightly and giggle.

"So how about a drink and celebrate a bit before they find us," Lacey whispers in a conspiratorial, hush-like tone.

"They find us?" I ask. I look around the hotel lobby, wondering if she's referring to my brother's guards.

"Yeah. My boss seems to think since my promotion that I'm his personal assistant at his beck and call. He can go fuck himself."

"That's cause you want him to fuck you," Casey teases.

Lacey slaps her arm and stomps her foot. "Bish, don't be calling me out like that just because he's fine as hell. The man has no idea I'm anything more than a workhorse. 'Lacey, do this. Lacey, do that.' I want to throat punch him."

"I think you like him bossing you around," I tease, making sure I'm out of slapping distance.

"Whatever. I need a drink now before he starts texting me about his meeting agenda that I'm totally ignoring because it's not due until Tuesday."

We walk into the bar and I immediately look for the men who walked in, but I don't see them. I'm not even sure why I care. It's not as if I have the balls to do something given that I'm a twenty-one-year-old virgin for a reason. It might be the fact that I have an overprotective older brother who has had guards watching over me since he could.

Tonight is special because we're celebrating Lacey's promotion at work and my graduation from a culinary program. It was an eighteen-month set of courses on baking, which I honestly didn't need but wanted.

Our waitress comes over and takes our order for a round of shots and three mixed drinks. I think that's going to be the totality of my drinking since I need to be up early and baking my heart out to earn a spot that I rightfully deserve with one of the top bakeries in the country.

"Girl, that guy over there hasn't taken his eyes off you," Casey says, dipping her head to the side. I can't see him unless I turn, and that would be completely obvious.

"What do you mean? What guy?"

"Mare, just go ahead and look to your left. Trust me—you won't be disappointed," Casey presses.

"That hot fucking guy sitting at the table with another man," Lacey agrees. I turn to my left and follow their gazes. Meeting his intent stare, I let out a gasp. Holy hell, it's the same man that I saw earlier and this time, he's the one staring at me. Goodness, the man is equally gorgeous from the front.

He has medium brown hair that's cut short and textured yet neat with the sides and back shorter. I want to run my hands through it, wondering if he looks even sexier with mussed-up locks. Suddenly the hotel bar has gotten twenty degrees hotter and a lot smaller. I rub the back of my neck under my long hair ever so slightly as if there's already sweat beginning to form.

He winks at me, and a blush spreads across my cheeks and I turn my head back to our table. "Come on, Mare, don't be shy. He looks like he could finally get you out of that situation you're in." She gives me a nudge with her elbow and wink.

I whip my head back at her. "It's not a situation. It's a choice." I roll my eyes at them, and I want to kick her shins with my heel.

"Choice or not. If you didn't have that hot brother breathing down your back for years, you wouldn't be a virgin now." Everyone reminds me that my brother's handsome, and he is, but he's finally married so he's gotten a little less overprotective of me.

"Now he hounds her."

"And since he's busy with his hot wife… maybe Mr. Obsessed over there can finally help you out," Casey adds. I sneak a sly peek behind my hair and see he's still staring. My pussy clenches, and I'm afraid that I'm going to make noise when I walk.

"I'm surprised your brother hasn't sent his minions to watch over you," Lacey brings up, looking around the room for the guys.

I use it as a distraction from the sexy beast at the other table. "I only have one at a time now because I'm an adult, but they keep their distance. I don't have people up my ass anymore. Besides, he knows I'm safe in the hotel and I'll call if I want to leave because they aren't far away."

"I'm betting *he* wants to be all up on your ass." She nods her head in the hot guy's direction.

"What has gotten into you tonight, Lace?" I lightly swat at her arm and shake my head, hoping to calm myself down because my heart's racing a million miles a minute to have that hot man all over me. I down my drink in one long gulp, needing some liquid courage to calm my nerves.

She giggles and takes a sip of her drink. "I don't know. Maybe it's because I'm happy. Now, go make us proud and accidentally drop something on the way to the ladies' room right in front of him." The waitress comes back as if she noticed we finished our drinks. We order another round even though I shouldn't be drinking so much.

Once she leaves, I continue the conversation. "Not going to happen. I don't have to go, and secondly, I have no intention of introducing myself. I'm not desperate." Okay, I'm not desperately waiting for any man, but suddenly my body is desperately craving his attention.

"Fine. You're going to miss out on a good thing, though."

"Doubt it. He's probably just looking to score like a vulture circling his next meal. Look what I'm wearing. I've picked one of the sluttiest outfits I could find for tonight."

"We noticed, and you look sexy as hell. No red-blooded male could miss that tempting display you've got going on. If I was a guy, I'd be panting like a dog in heat around you." She winks and then licks her chops at me.

"This isn't me, though. He won't want the real me in the morning."

"Honey, please. Besides, this isn't about forever, anyway. If you're going to lose your virginity, you might as well lose it to a guy like that instead of that one guy that follows you around at school."

Casey tilts her head toward the handsome guy across the bar and adds, "At least that guy looks like he'll make you come." She has no idea that I'm already halfway there, but I don't need to give them any more ammo.

"I told you. Damon and I were just classmates. We never hung out outside of class hours. Hell, he doesn't even have my number. Besides, it's not like I'm interested in him. It wouldn't happen, so there's no presumptive comparison."

"Girl, that guy has it bad for you. I'm glad you graduated so he'll stop following you around like a puppy dog."

"Actually, we're both applying to the same place. Tomorrow's the baking challenge at this hotel. Only the best will be up for the job, so that's why I need your support," I remind them just as the waitress sets down another round of drinks. We pass them around and cheer.

Lacey raises her glass. "Of course, Mare. You're going to nail it tomorrow. You're the best baker anyone has ever seen. Seriously, the judges aren't going to know what hit them, and they'll be begging you to join their bakery. Cheers."

"Cheers," Casey and I say, clinking our glasses before taking a drink.

"Wait—didn't your brother offer to buy you your own bakery?" Casey asks.

"Yes, he did, but of course I turned him down. I want to be a big girl and prove myself."

"Marilyn, you don't have shit to prove. It would be a wise investment for him because you'd make it a hit."

"Still, I need to do this and see if I can handle the pressure before I waste his money."

"Fine, but have another drink and then hit up that fine-ass motherfucker before you go to bed." I look his way, and as if he feels my eyes on him, he turns his head toward me.

A part of me is tempted to follow the girls' plan, but I'm just not that crazy confident.

Suddenly there's a shadow at the table followed by a deep growl. Strangely, it doesn't affect me like I've read in the books, and then I hear Lacey say, "Mr. Hardwick." I glance and see it's her boss. Lacey's eyes widen, and her pulse picks up along the carotid artery in her neck.

"Up out of that seat now, Lacey," he tells her.

"No. You're not the boss of my free time, mister." She tries to act tough, but it's like a little kitten who thinks they're a tiger. It's adorable.

"What the fuck are you wearing?" he snarls when he can see down her dress. Her rack is pretty nice and clearly on display.

"It's a dress. I'm sure you've seen one before. We all have them."

"I'm not going to tell you again to get up."

She smiles sweetly at him. "Good, because I'm not done with my drink."

He growls, and she sips her drink fast, knowing damn well he's going to be taking her out of her seat. The smirk she gives me is almost too much to bear, but I hold in my smile when I feel another body moving closer to us.

CHAPTER

Two

JULIEN

The bar is already crowded from what I can see as I stand outside of it, and I'm regretting the decision to meet down here.

We could have met in my hotel room instead of coming all the way down here; I'm not comfortable in crowds, but since my brother got the records for me, he took pleasure in torturing me with this request.

"Stop scowling, bro. It's not even that busy inside the bar." He chuckles as he looks at the place and then back at me. Honestly, it's not that busy yet, but I still don't care for it. To me, it's too much to deal with and I hate it.

"Shut it, George," I grumble through clenched

teeth, walking into the bar area of the hotel and finding a table off to the side near the door. "Let's take a seat right here." I want to a spot to make a quick escape as soon as we finish up.

"Sounds good to me. I've brought all the documents you asked for." My assistant was supposed to do it, but he flaked out on me, claiming he misunderstood my instructions, leaving the prepared documents on my desk. Finding good help is hard these days.

I unbutton my suit jacket and sit down while George pulls out his satchel. "How many candidates do we have for tomorrow? I'm tired of going through all these without skill or work ethic." My assistant immediately comes to mind.

He sets the files on the table. "These are the batch that are doing the bake-off tomorrow at this hotel. All of them are talented, high marks in school." It's a small stack of manilla folders. I haven't had time to look at them sooner because I have three bakeries across the Chicagoland area and my schedule is jammed packed.

"But the true test will be how they handle the pressure," I tell him. That is always the most challenging part for these kids. It takes more than mixing ingredients; love for the art has to be in it to make it work.

"Hello, gentlemen. What can I get you to drink?" our waitress asks, standing a little too close to me. Fuck, I can't stand when people are nearby. I twist my chair, scooting it slightly back away from her.

"We'll both have a Modelo. Right, sweetheart?" George says to me, putting his hand on mine, rubbing it back and forth softly. He's the only one I let get away with it because he's my brother and knows me too damn well.

"Yes, dear," I answer, smiling tenderly at him.

"Always the super-hot ones," she huffs, walking away from us. I hold back a laugh and sit back in my seat, but not before smacking his hand.

"That never gets old. God, one of these days you've got to get used to women flirting with you—or men, if that's the case."

"It's not the case."

He throws his hands up just to make sure I'm not offended, which I'm not because I'm sure he's had questions over the years. "It's cool, bro. Either way, I'm still your brother and happy to be your deflector."

"Thanks. How about we go over these files so I know what I'm looking for tomorrow?"

"You want to show up late and avoid meeting the

bakers and just taste their desserts, don't you?" He knows me all too well.

"It's all I'm there for." I don't want to take part in the media spectacle or the small talk between the competitors. I have so many competitors who will watch my every move and trying to pick the one I'm vying for only because I want them.

"You know they do have to work side by side with you, so you'll have to like them a little." It's a fair point that he's making, but it becomes too crazy to get to know these people, anyway.

"Yes, but not all of them will be there. Besides, it's not so much the bakers that bother me; it's all the assistants and managers talking and wanting to speak with me, trying to pick my brain, steal my recipes."

"Julien, it was one time." You only need one good betrayal in your life never to trust a motherfucker again. There are sayings about that shit for a reason.

"Yes, and the bastard made a fortune on it." When I worked for my first bakery, I was just sixteen and I'd come up with a fantastic dessert and the owner stole the recipe, claimed it as his, and then sold it commercially, making a killing.

At that age I had no financial recourse, so I held my head up high and kept my mouth shut. Maybe that's why I don't like people. "And we have completely crushed him financially. We're three times wealthier than him, so he can go fuck himself."

Our waitress returns with our drinks and says, "Here you go, fellas. Please let me know if you need anything else."

"Thanks. We're good for now." He winks at her, and she smiles because my brother, even pretending to be my boyfriend, is still a charmer. We're the exact opposite, and maybe that's why we work so great together as a team.

"Excuse me. We've just gotten a lively crowd in." I look over to the area she pointed to, hoping to avoid the crowd and thinking maybe we'll go somewhere else, like back to my hotel room. However, the second my eyes land on the women, one in particular, I've changed my mind.

I'm not going anywhere with George. I'm following that beautiful creature wherever she'll lead me, even if it's to hell and back, because I found my other half. *All this time.*

I stare at the woman in a little black dress. She smiles as she takes a seat and her lips curve genuinely toward the hostess who seats her. Scanning the table, the rest of her party is all women, which is good. If another man had been there, I'd have to break his jaw.

"Earth to Julien, tuck your damn tongue back in

your mouth. You look like a wolf cartoon character right now." I feel wolfish, and she's my prey. I'd love to eat her up from head to toe, stopping to enjoy her creamy center.

"I don't have my tongue out," I grunt, waiting for her to look my way. I argue the irrelevant point because I'm sure I come off as a crazy man, but none of that matters. I've found my other half and she will be mine.

"Yes, but you haven't taken your eyes off that group of women. It's not like you. What's going on, Julien?"

"I found my future wife." The words fall effortlessly from my lips.

"Future wife? You don't know those women. Hell, I don't even know which of them you're talking about."

"The beauty in the black dress," I answer while keeping my eyes on her.

"Lord, that narrowed it down." He slaps his hand down on the table with disbelief in his voice. I just ignore him because she's all that matters. I want her and I will have her.

"The one that refuses to look at me," I growl, intensifying my stare, willing her to look at me.

"Ah, I sense some negative karma." He chuckles,

knowing my antisocial ass is getting a taste of my own medicine.

"Shut up. She doesn't even know that she's become mine." But the reality will soon hit her.

"What if she's got a man?" It's a question that pisses me off, but I have a simple solution.

"She's not wearing a ring, so I guess he doesn't fucking matter to me. And if there is some asshole, he won't be *matter* at all." Because I'll make him disappear.

"Wow, what the hell happened to my dickhead, quiet brother who hates people?" He laughs as he says it.

"That hasn't changed. She's the exception." I continue to stare at her, absorbing her pure aura, craving this woman unlike anything I've ever known before. She sweeps her long, dark hair off her shoulder, revealing that luscious pale skin I want to bite.

"I think you've lost it. No. As a matter of fact, I know you've lost it."

"No, I've found it." I grab my drink and guzzle it before setting it down with feeling before standing and adjusting my suit. My cock's stiffer than my drink, making me more and more anxious to meet my wife-to-be.

"Julien, we still have to go over the candidates," he reminds me, his voice sounding annoyingly whiny.

"Fuck the candidates," I snarl through clenched teeth. I straighten my suit jacket and then walk toward her table just as a large man approaches seconds before me.

Jealousy like I've never experienced in my entire life floods my every bone and I'm ready to lose my mind. I'm about to knock his ass out, but he quickly grabs the blonde friend and flips her over his shoulder, eliminating one problem.

"Idiot, put me down," she squeals with a giggle at the end. He just grunts a "no" and carries her away. She calls out, "Look who's here to see you, Mare. Remember what I said. He's fine as hell." The guy swats her ass.

My woman's eyes dart straight in my direction, ending up right at my crotch and then moving upward. "Hello, I'm Julien Beaumont."

"She's Marilyn Shaw, a virgin, and it's time for me to go. See ya, girl. Let me know how it goes." The other friend stands and walks away.

I take the vacated seat because I have no intention of giving this beautiful woman an opportunity to leave as well, especially given the very private information her friend just divulged.

I sit up straight and stare at her, trying to calm my racing heart. "So, Marilyn, it seems we're finally alone."

She looks around the room, but I want her eyes back on me. Thankfully, she doesn't take long. "Not quite. It looks like we're in a room full of people, Julien." Fuck me. Is she tempting me with her pursed red lips? The way she said my name. Fuck. It was like a sensual kiss on my cock.

I reach out and take her hand in mine, feeling her soft fingers under my larger ones. Electricity shoots through the tips all the way to my heart. Fuck, I need to have her soon or I'm going to lose it. "If we go back to my hotel room, I'm not sure you'll be a virgin by the end of the night."

Her body fills with tension and then she asks, "Are you married?"

Shaking my head slightly, I look into her dark brown eyes. I answer her honestly. "No." Well, based on the question she asked. Not the question in my head. Because I will be married soon… to her.

"Then maybe I don't want to be a virgin anymore," she confesses. I groan as my dick swells against my gray slacks, stretching the expensive material. It better prove its worth and hold until I get her alone.

"Well, that's where we have a problem, ma chérie. I'm not just interested in fucking you for a night." I want forever, and I will have it.

"Well, maybe that's all that you'll get." She sassily twists her lips before taking one more sip from her drink.

Standing up, I pull out my wallet and drop a hundred-dollar bill on the table for the waitress. "We'll see about that." Taking her hand and dragging her out of her seat, I lead her out of the hotel bar. My brother watches in shock, mouth open, but he doesn't say a word.

CHAPTER

Three

MARILYN

We reach the bank of elevators, and he hits the up button just before he pins me to the wall. His waist firmly against my core, grinding into mine. "I'm going to kiss you now, Marilyn." He's not asking for permission. It's a warning, but I don't need one.

"Please," I beg, needing that sensuous-looking mouth on mine. His gray eyes darken as he drops his head and his lips crush mine as our eyes close.

"The elevator," someone says beside us. Julien has me tucked so tightly to him I can't see who it is; however, the muffled voice sounds vaguely familiar.

I'm grateful I can't tell who it is, and hopefully they can't see me.

"Oh," Julien grunts, pulling back and taking my hand to lead me inside. He doesn't bother looking at the person and then hits the button for the top floor.

"I'll wait for the next one," the guy says.

Julien doesn't wait for the doors to close before I'm against the wall and his mouth is on mine, dominating me. I moan, crying out as I grind my hips on his hard ridge. The thick meat between his legs pulses against my core, and he pushes harder.

"I need to be inside you." The doors open, and he scoops me up in his big, strong arms, carrying me out of the elevator and then to his suite. He kicks the door closed with his foot and then puts me down on the sofa.

His hands slide up my thighs, fingers flexing, gripping my muscles roughly and mashing them as he feels his way to my ass. We rock and grind, kissing violently until he pulls his lips away with a growl.

"Fuck, you're made for me."

"Julien," I breathe, moaning as he ducks his head down and his tongue dips along my throat. "I need you to take me."

"I am, and I'm never giving you back." His fingers work my zipper down my back, pausing to slide his hands along my bare skin. "So smooth. I want to strip you and lick every inch and see if you taste sweet everywhere."

"There's only one way to find out," I challenge.

My behavior foolish and reckless since I've no experience, but there's just something about this man that sends every hormone in my body into overdrive. I don't know if it's the girls' words or his, but all I want is for him to take me until there is no innocence left in me.

Tugging down one strap and then the other, he lowers my dress, revealing my breasts that ache in a new way. "Wow, so perfect, Marilyn." His hand wraps around one breast, squeezing it as he sucks my nipple into his mouth, grazing it with his pearly white teeth.

"Julien, I need more. Don't stop." I grip his hair and run my fingers through it, feeling the thick, silky strands. I need his clothes off too, so I tug at his jacket. "I need to feel you against me, please."

"No need to beg, but it does sound like music from your lips." He kisses me quickly before standing, sliding off his suit jacket and then going for his tie. I watch him as his eyes linger on my chest and his tongue swipes along his lips. "Strip and show me your sweet cookie." My pussy heats up at his words, gushing all over my silky red panties. "It's all mine, and I want it now." I stare, mesmerized as he undoes his slacks that are barely containing his monster of a cock inside.

I lick my lips, wondering when I became such a nympho given I've never been with a man. Reaching out, I grab his cock through his boxer briefs and let my knees hit the carpet. "I wanna lick the lollipop."

"Just one lick, my beauty." I shove down his boxers and that massive length bounces free. I'm not sure I can do more than lick it, but I suddenly feel like a bad girl. Gripping his girth at the base, I lick from the edge of my hand to the tip where a bead of cream is waiting for me, but I don't pull away. No, I wrap my lips around his engorged head, sucking on his thick pole. A guttural moan rips through him, and my pussy flutters at his nonverbal praise.

He grips my hair, pulling it hard, yanking me off his cock so fast I have dribble coming off my lips. "You're a bad girl. I told you just one lick."

I smile up at him with an arched brow and a smart-ass attitude, knowing he's beyond turned on. "It was only one lick. You didn't say I couldn't suck it."

"You're going to learn to do what I say, my beauty." Hunger and lust darken his eyes as he kicks off his shoes and then tugs off his boxers with his pants before he steps closer with his massive cock and taps it on my lips. "Open up. Time to take orders."

I'm nearly coming on the spot from what's to come. I run my fingers between my thighs, slipping them under my panties. I give him my mouth like a good girl, and he slides his length inside, pushing it in a couple of inches, but he's too much for me to take so he slowly pulls out and then in again.

Repeatedly, he fucks my mouth until he growls and pulls completely out without coming. He bends down and presses his mouth roughly to mine. "You look so sexy with lips so thoroughly fucked, but my cum is for your pussy."

He takes my hand from my panties and then brings my fingers to his lips, sucking each one. "Pussy's finger-licking good, but I'm going to need to sample straight from the source." Lifting me up like I'm a feather, he carries me to the bed in just my heels and panties.

My heart's pounding out of my chest, and I look at him and know that this isn't just some fling for me. Even though we've just met, I feel a connection to him. It's not love, because that would be crazy. Lust? Hell, yes, but it's like maybe we can have more than tonight.

I cup his face and say, "Promise me you're not married."

He kisses my nose before looking at me with sincerity in his eyes. "I promise, Marilyn. Until tonight, I didn't know there was someone I'd ever want to wake up next to." Before I can respond, his mouth lands on mine, silencing any response.

Julien moves down my body, kissing my mons over the silly daisy panties I slipped on. "*Ma marguerite*, I feel like a lucky man." His blunt fingers grip the hem of my panties and slide them down my legs. "Let me get rid of these. As sexy as they are, I only want you wearing my sweat and cum."

He delves his talented tongue between my slit, licking and sucking on my juicy hole until I'm screaming his name.

"We can stop now if you'd like, Marilyn."

"Have you changed your mind?" I ask, hoping he doesn't want to quit because I need to feel him possess me completely.

"Not one bit. I want to be inside more than anything, but I won't rush you, no matter what I said earlier," he grunts, running his hands over my smooth legs.

"Well, I need you in me. I want you inside me. Julien, take me."

"Fair warning—you're mine." We kiss again before he presses the tip of his thick cock through my slit.

Slowly he stretches me, inch by inch until he hits the last strands of my innocence, tearing it to shreds. I let out a mixed cry and moan as the pain and pleasure intertwine.

"I'm sorry, my beauty." He stills, trying to remain calm as I take him all the way.

"I'm fine. You're just so big," I say shakily. My fingernails grip his biceps, holding onto them as I adjust to the pain of his intrusion.

As I get used to it, I loosen my fingers and slide my hands over his broad shoulders and into his hair, bringing his head down to mine.

We share a deep kiss, tongues gliding together, mimicking the act of sex before I beg him to continue making love to me.

"Please, I need you, Julien."

"I thought you'd never ask," he growls, grinding his hips, rolling them as we move gently. Sweat building along our bodies, the sheets becoming entangled with legs.

"You feel so good around my cock." He rocks forward, fucking my pussy slowly, working in and out.

"I think I'm going to come," I moan, feeling that insane pleasure building. His lips wrap around my fat nipple, sucking on my breast until I'm coming.

With a pop, he releases my breast and then roars, shooting his load deep inside me; filling me up with his seed until it's dripping out between us.

Gasping and breathing heavily, he rolls onto his back with his arms around me, cradling me close. "That was amazing," he groans.

I brush my lips against his shoulder and then rest my head only to hear him whisper, "Mine."

I wake up with the realization of what I've done. My brain is telling me I should be filled with regret for sleeping with a stranger and giving him my virginity, but I don't. I only regret that I need to be somewhere else in an hour.

Turning my head, I see Julien's handsome face unbothered, relaxed. It almost makes me want to forget all I've worked to prove, but I can't. My body protests as it wants to stay put in his strong arms, wanting to lay wrapped up with this man until the end of time. Unfortunately, life doesn't work that way.

Steeling my spine, I quickly and quietly slither out

of his bed and gather my clothes. Fuck, my zipper won't go up. I grab his dress shirt and put it over me and walk out of the hotel room with my things, stealing one glance back at the most handsome man I've ever met.

My chest aches as I make my way to the elevator. I should have told him what my room number is or at least given him my number. I'm not going to be around for the whole day, and I don't know when he's leaving.

Even if he said he wants forever last night, I know it could have been just all talk, but that doesn't mean we couldn't see each other one more time. Maybe… we could have a relationship. I'll try to come back up here after the challenge is over.

Still, I am preparing for the bake-off, where five companies will be there to look at all of us to see if any of us meet their standards.

Once I'm in my room, I shower and change into my clothes for the competition, pinning up my hair into a tight ponytail. I see the faint marks that Julien left on my skin as he made me cry out his name. Using some cover up and concealer, I hide the blemishes and head down to the area for the bake-off.

I get downstairs and into the kitchen area with all the other candidates when I see the man who had been sitting with Julien standing there with a tablet in his hand.

His eyes meet mine, and a broad smile spreads over his face because he knows a secret everyone else in the room doesn't.

My eyes scan the room, but I don't see Julien anywhere. What if he's one of the other bakers? What if he's one of the employers?

JULIEN

The sound of the door clicking shut wakes me from the best night of my life. I know she's left me and I have seconds to catch her, so I'm on my feet, slipping on my boxer briefs and running out of the room.

Damn it, the weight of my dumbass decision hits me when I feel my door close behind me. Fuck. I don't have anything on me, not even my cell phone nor my room keycard as I stand in the middle of the empty hallway. I press the button for the elevator that had just closed before I stepped fully out of my room. It takes a moment for it to make its way back up.

However, once it comes up, I press the emergency stop and call button.

Seconds later, a male voice answers, "Hello, how can we help you?"

"I'm Julien Beaumont, staying in the penthouse suite, and I've locked myself out of my room."

"You can come down to the lobby and get another key, sir."

"I'm not quite dressed, so if you could send up one of your male employees to let me in. All of my identification is inside the room."

"We'll send someone up in a moment." I could almost hear the laughter on the other end as they hung up. Fucking asshole.

I wait against the wall because there is another penthouse suite up here and I don't want them to come out of their room and see me in my underwear. Not that my body isn't cut with rippling muscle, but I hate to have people look at me. It's how I've managed to stay out of the limelight even though I own one of the world's most successful bakeries and two world-class restaurants.

A man comes up with a tablet and notices my predicament. "Hello, sir. Let me get you back inside."

"That's it? There's no verification?" I don't like the lack of security in this hotel.

"Sir, when you called, we looked up the security footage to the moment right before you called down. We noticed that a young lady had left. It's clear you came from the room and you're the sole occupant. Did she rob you?"

"No. I mean… not that I would know, but that's not why I was trying to bring her back. Can you assist me with locating her?"

"I'm sorry, sir, but she got off on another floor and because she's a guest, I can't provide any of that information. It would be a violation of privacy, and we could be sued."

"I'll find her myself," I snarl, wanting to deck the fucker for being almost useless.

"This time, I suggest you put on some clothes after gathering your keycard," he remarks, looking down at my body.

"Oh, yes. Damn, she has me all messed up," I grunt, stepping into the room and closing the door behind him. I need to get ready to locate that woman. My phone rings on the floor somewhere. I dig around and find it, only to have missed a call from my brother.

George shoots me a text: *I hope you're in the damn elevator because the bake-off starts in thirty minutes.*

Son of a bitch. I don't give a fuck about the bake-off. I need to find my woman and demand she tell me why she ran from me. She gave me her virginity, let me fill her with my seed, and then just took off as soon as the sun was up.

After a quick shower, I clean up my clothes from yesterday and realize that *ma marguerite* stole more than my heart—my favorite dress shirt is gone too. I'm going to have to spank her ass good when I find her and then fuck her holes so good she doesn't want to leave again.

My phone goes off again, so I swipe it off the dresser and answer my brother's call. "Why are you harassing me?"

"Because you're late, and you're never late."

"I had a little problem. Take notes for me, and I'll be there soon."

"There are people down here that are waiting for you."

"You know I hate people."

"Not all people. Did you lose your… last night?" he asks like the asshole he is. I will choke him when I get a chance, but for now, all I want to do is find her.

"Mind your business. I'm coming."

"I hope you did as well last night, and I'm not talking about a solo job."

"Shut it, George. I'm on my way down. Also, we need someone who's willing to get me information on a guest staying at the hotel," I say.

"Stop focusing on her and get down here. That's what you got my ass down for in the first place when I have so many other better things to do."

I grumble and end the call, tucking my phone in my suit jacket pocket. After fixing my tie, I gather my keycard, my portfolio case, keys, and wallet, and step out of the room. At least this time I'm dressed.

The entire elevator ride seems to take forever as people step on. Still, it gives me a chance to see if she gets on. Unfortunately, by the time I reached the lobby, she hadn't climbed aboard. I exit with a scowl that sends people running in the opposite direction.

"Ah, Mr. Beaumont. The bakers have already arrived at their stations and are set up to bake several treats of their own preference with the limited ingredients given," Gretchen says, walking up to me. She's the receptionist for the office and here on behalf of George to take notes.

I step inside the kitchen setup that is larger than I expected. The room is packed with ten different employers looking for the best along with their staff and the hosts of this special event, the local culinary school. Still, none of that matters when I see who I've been thinking about from the second she slipped from my arms this morning. Marilyn is standing behind one of the working stations.

A young man is speaking with her, and he's a little too close for my liking. Doesn't he realize that she belongs to me? Ma marguerite screamed my name all night long after I ripped through her innocence. I walk past all the other potential employers, seeing my brother standing there with a smirk on his smug face. I wink at him and then walk straight up to her station.

"*Ma marguerite*, so what will you be making me today?" She gasps and nearly stumbles backward, but I grab her by her elbow, catching her. It's clear that my identity takes her by surprise.

"Julien, you're one of the employers."

I shake my head because there's no way I'd let her work for anyone else. "No, I'm now your employer. You may finish your dessert, but you will be working alongside me."

"You don't even know if I'm a good fit."

A grin spreads over my face. "That is a lie. I know you are. I believe we were a great fit."

"Excuse me, but she's trying to bake here."

"Who is he, Marilyn?" I growl, staring down at the thinner young guy who is clearly trying to insert himself between Marilyn and me. That's not going to happen because not a soul will come between us.

"This is my classmate Damon."

"Then shouldn't you be at your own station and away from her?" I snarl at him. He backs up.

"Watch it, Lynny. He's after more than just your cookies." I shrug, and she smiles while shaking her head as Damon walks back to his station.

I lean in and whisper, "I've had your cookie, and I want more. So is this why you disappeared?"

"Yes, but can we talk about this later?" she insists.

"I suppose, but this doesn't mean you're going to work for anyone else but me."

She waves her hands toward me, shooing me away, but it will do her no good. "Well, let me do my thing and you can go back to your busy schedule. It will take me about forty-five minutes."

"I'll stay and watch."

"Okay. The pressure's on." She smiles and then gets to work, doing her best to ignore the hovering I'm doing. I can't help myself. It has nothing to do with the fact that she's trying out for the job. In fact, everyone gets a simple baking task. A simple peanut butter cookie or a brownie recipe from scratch, and if they present it as I expect, then I give them a chance —but I simply want to watch her in action.

She moves delicately yet rapidly, effortlessly mixing, and I see she's making cupcakes. "Do you have any allergies, Chef Beaumont?"

"Julien. And no, I don't have any," I remind her. After all, I've eaten more than just her baked goodies.

"Good. I think you'll like these. It's been a long time since I've made these, but depending on how fancy the event or what other desserts or dishes are served, it can be revised."

"Hello, Julien. Long time no see." I turn and see Vanessa Sims, another baker who wanted more than a lesson in making soufflés with me, but she didn't understand that I don't like people.

"For good reason, and it's Mr. Beaumont."

Marilyn gasps with her mouth open. "Always so prudish. How can a man like you resist beauty?"

"Ms. Shaw, will you excuse me? I must check on the other candidates." I quickly move away from her before I say something rude.

CHAPTER
Five

MARILYN

"You're wasting your time flirting with the man. I'm guessing he has something wrong with him in that department." I'm about to teach this bitch some manners, but it's clear she's just salty. It's hilarious that for a moment I was actually jealous.

"Thank you for the unsolicited advice, but I need to finish working on my desserts, and Chef Beaumont's affairs aren't appropriate for discussion."

"Obviously you want to work for him, but honey, he's hard to please."

"Vanessa, it's good to see you again," the guy who was with Julien yesterday says.

"George, what is wrong with your brother?" she

asks him so rudely, but her blatant ignorance erases some of my own. I know who he is now.

"There's nothing wrong with my brother. He just doesn't deal with fake people, and you're faker than artificial flavoring." I clamp my lips together, fighting off a laugh.

"Damn, Georgie, I thought you were sweeter than that bitter bitch." She sashays away.

"Oh, no. I guess I've lost her as a potential employer," I say with a giggle, pressing my hand to my lips.

"Like Julien would let you go anywhere he isn't." I watch him speaking to another woman across from me, but I know she's a great baker and a married mother of two. Still, a twinge of jealousy shoots through me. It's irrational and silly, but it still does.

"I doubt it. He hasn't tasted anything I've made yet."

"First, I have your records just like all the employers here, so I know that on paper you're the most qualified candidate. Second, that man would take you if you didn't know the oven from the damn cabinet. I've never seen my brother like that last night."

"Thanks for that. We both must not have been

acting like ourselves. Excuse me, I need to finish making these cupcakes before I run out of time."

"I told you, you're working for me," Julien says, coming up to stand next to his brother. His eyes darken with intent as his voice deepens with each syllable. My panties are drenched under the yoga pants that I'd decided to wear for the competition. Although this is like a job interview, our clothes aren't meant to be formal. It's about being presentable while comfortable in the kitchen, and nothing screams flexibility and comfort like a great pair of stretchy black yoga pants that allow me to bend and move around effortlessly.

"That doesn't mean I'm not still going to put out a great product. I take my skills extremely seriously." I glare at him, giving him a warning not to press the issue. I'm already on edge with Julien and then that damn woman came along. From their frosty greeting I thought they were ex-lovers, but then it was clear he just can't stand her and she doesn't like it. She'd definitely been mistaken about his virility.

He throws his hands up. "Fine, I'll stand here and watch."

"I think we need to check out the other candidates as well. You need at least two qualified ones for the major event."

He shakes his head and crosses his muscular arms over his thick, muscled chest, staring at me as he speaks to his brother. "I know that, and I've already visited three stations. I will wait until it's time to test every dessert."

Another one of the employers steps up to my table where I'm trying to prepare my icings. "Hello, Miss Shaw. I've been anxious to try your desserts. I've heard they're the best."

"I wouldn't say that, but I put a lot of effort into them."

"You're welcome to have a sample when they're done, but Miss Shaw has already been offered a spot at my bakery and has accepted."

"I haven't accepted anything. Now, gentlemen, if you'll please excuse me, I need to finish working."

"We'll see about that," Julien growls.

"Of course, Miss Shaw," George says and then takes his brother by the elbow, guiding him away, even though Julien refuses to take his eyes off me until he has no choice.

The other man turns to Damon's station to watch him work. That's when I notice that Damon's working hard. I return my attention to my cupcakes, which are insanely important to me even if Julien demands I work for him.

It's probably not going to be a long employment. Couples rarely make it working together. I consider my brother and his wife the exception and not the rule. Then again, they've only been married for a couple of months.

For the next twenty minutes, I create some cupcake decorations before taking the cupcakes out of the oven to put them on the cooling racks. Once they're set in the freezer, I come back to making my cupcake designs and step on something squishy. Looking down at my foot, I see my green icing smeared all over. One of my pastry bags must have fallen on the floor when I was rushing to put everything in the fridge.

After taking five minutes to clean up the mess, I have to prep a much smaller piping bag with the rest of the green icing I prepared that didn't end up ruined. Finally, I pull out the cupcakes and the flower toppers I made out of icing. Then I pipe on some icing to adhere them to the cooled tops. For the finishing touch, I added a few more flowers and leaves to each before plating the twenty-four cupcakes I was required to make.

"You should be careful, Lynny. He's a player. Last night he was all over some whore in an elevator. She was in a tight dress and moaning wildly, so he's just gonna screw you and leave." So it was Damon outside the elevator.

"Thanks," I mutter, bending down into the cabinet below, pretending to look for something in an attempt to hide the blush.

"These are beautiful, ma marguerite." I don't know why he calls me that or what it means, but he's called me that randomly since last night. It means something, and when I get a chance, I will look it up.

"Thank you," I blush and raise my gaze to Julien to see his eyes laser-focused on my mouth like he's ready to pounce around the metal table that stands between us.

Several of the employers arrive at my station to sample my desserts now that my treats have been set out.

"So what are the flavors?" Mrs. Collins asks, stepping forward to examine the design on them. She's an older woman with pinned-back gray hair. From her name tag, I can see she's from a bakery in New Lenox.

"We have a red velvet with a cream-cheese filling, and this one here is a peanut butter chocolate cupcake."

"They look too good to bite into," another voice

utters, and that's when I recognize a baker from Michigan Ave.

"Thank you. I made them in a rush today, but I've been working on the recipe for years." Julien is the first to grab a fork and peel the wrapping. Stabbing through the beautiful design with the side of his utensil, he splits the cake to see the interior. "The texture is perfect." Making sure to get every section on his fork, Julien brings it to his mouth and bites down. A moan escapes involuntarily, and I do my best to fight my own whimper. The way his throat moves, I want to reach over and lick that strong column.

"The flavor of the red velvet, which isn't usually a favorite, has been moved up. I can taste every flavor. Now, it's time for the other one," he growls, slicing his fork into the next one.

"I thought I loved the first one, but damn, the second is even better," Mr. Greenway from Michigan Ave Bakery says. It's then that I realize that everyone else has grabbed cupcakes. I'd been so wrapped up in watching the way Julien ate my cupcake, I missed several others taking a sample.

"You're hired, Miss Shaw," Julien states in front of everyone else, leaving no room for them to argue as they swallow their bite down.

"Yay. Are you serious?" I ask, wondering if he really enjoyed my cupcakes.

"Yes. It seems you live up to your hype. I'm glad to have you join my team."

"Thank you. I'm so excited. When do I start?" A bunch of downtrodden faces and a couple of groans come from around me.

"When it doesn't work out, you can have a position at my bakery."

"Same here, Miss Shaw. Here's my card," Mr. Greenway offers, handing me a business card, but Julien snatches it from my fingers and hands it to his brother.

"Deal with that," he orders.

"Yes, Julien." His brother holds back a laugh.

"Congratulations, Miss Shaw. Now that you've finished and have nailed a spot like I expected, you can leave at any time," my former school director says. "The staff will clean up the kitchen area." They don't want us wandering to the other candidates' stations because they don't want any stealing of ideas or assisting.

"Thank you. I need to call my brother." He will be so proud of me.

"What's your room number?" Julien asks.

"313, but I'm actually checked out already."

"I will be looking for you."

"Do you need me to fill out some forms?"

"Yes, fill this out." George hands me his tablet. I grab the tablet and fill out a quick two-page employment form. "The rest of the paperwork can be done at the office."

I leave the hotel, feeling a vast array of emotions. I'm brimming with excitement and smiling from ear to ear so much that I'm home without remembering the short drive. Between last night's wild, dirty encounter to this morning's shocking and successful performance, I'm vibrating with energy.

As soon as I toss my purse on the sofa, I dial my brother's number. I know it's during his workday and he's busy, but he wanted me to call and I can't wait.

He answers, and without missing a beat, says, "How did it go?"

"I got the job," I squeal, practically dancing around the room.

"What? Congratulations. I knew you would. So when do you start?"

"Tomorrow."

"That's pretty quick." I don't like that switch in his tone. "What company are you working for?"

"I'm working for Julien Beaumont and his bakeries, *Les Frères*."

"Do you mean the man you were seen at the hotel with last night?" he says.

"How did you…? Never mind." I already know the answer. Even though he's given me some distance, his security isn't entirely gone. "That's none of your business."

"I'm your brother. I care about you, and I don't like this."

"Why?"

"Because he's only hiring you to get in your pants." Yes, I'm livid as can be. He's already been in my pants. He doesn't need to hire me for that.

"Oh, hell, no! What the fuck? Jack, I can't even believe you. You of all people should fucking talk. I can't even. I just can't. Thanks, bro." I hang up on my brother because there's no way in hell I can talk to him right now, maybe ever. I pace back and forth before collapsing on my sofa.

I can't believe he'd say something like that. Not that he's not completely wrong. Julien and I crossed every single professional boundary until I was screaming his name a couple of times, but I earned my place as a baker as well. Why the fuck does it matter that we're attracted to each other? I'm a fabulous baker. I'm incredible, and Jack should know it. He was willing to pay for my own bakery. Then again, maybe Jack only wanted to do it so I'd feel better and was trying to take care of me. For all I know, he'd probably have a standing company order to keep me in business.

Tears stream down my face while I sit on my sofa, letting my head fall back against the headrest as the joy of today fades away. I can't believe I was so proud of myself. The shame of sleeping with my boss hits me. I run into the bathroom and strip down, showering off his scent, but I can't erase his touch.

My phone rings on the cushion next to me. I scoop it up only to see Jack's name, so I send it to voicemail. Seconds later it rings again, so I send it to voicemail and then this time, I turn it off. He has nothing to say to me that I want to listen to.

I cry myself into a deep sleep, letting the weight of today seep through my bones.

JULIEN

After spending another hour in the bake-off tasting other desserts and debating on other candidates, I selected one other to join my team: a married woman who I was introduced to at the beginning of the day. Her skills are nearly up there with my dear Marilyn who is an expert in baking. I cannot believe that not only did I meet my soul mate, but that she is also a magician in the kitchen as well.

I'm just about to walk out with George by my side when that fuck from earlier comes up to me. "You've messed with the wrong girl. Lynny's mine, and I've worked really hard to nail her. I won't let it be ruined just so she can advance her career. Why don't you go back to that whore you had last night?"

"Boy, I will destroy you." I'm about to swing at him when my brother holds me back.

"Remember where we are, Julien. You have to get back to your woman. Ignore this asshole. She's your girl now, and he's only huffing and puffing because he can't have her."

"You're right." I brush off my brother's hold and look right at that smug asshole and say, "She's mine —she knows it, I know it, and everyone who could hear her calling my name last night knows it, so stay away from her or I'll end you." I walk out because I need to hold ma beauté.

We check out of my hotel room twenty minutes later, and I have everything loaded into my SUV and then George drives me over to her apartment where I see a handsome bastard in a suit walking up her steps.

I move right past him as his phone rings and he stops to answer it. I knock on her door but she doesn't answer, so I pound hard. "Ma chèrie, open up."

"Julien?" I hear her sweet voice that cracks, and I wonder what the fuck is wrong and who this asshole is. How many men do I have to fend off this delicate creature in a given day? It doesn't matter as I'll send them all running because she's mine.

"Ma chèrie, it's me."

"One moment," she says before I hear the lock unclick.

"What the fuck are you doing here?" the asshole next to me growls, attempting to challenge me, but he doesn't have a clue that before I became one of the world's best bakers, my brother and I grew up on the streets fighting for scraps—quite literally.

"None of your business, and who the fuck are you?" I practically spit out, ready to beat him down as the door opens.

"Her brother."

Marilyn yanks and pulls me into her apartment by my collar and slams the door in her brother's face. "Jack, go home. You didn't have to rush over here because I didn't answer your phone call."

"Rush? You're my sister, if you haven't forgotten?" He's the one who has forgotten since he's the ass that upset her.

"I think you have. Besides, I don't want to talk to you. Please leave." She presses her head into my chest.

"You heard her." I do my best to control the anger because she needs me.

"Fine, but we're not done talking about this." His footsteps get softer as he leaves.

"What are you doing here, Julien?" she asks.

"I missed you." A smile forms on her gorgeous face. "Besides, I told you we have things to discuss."

"Julien, you don't have to hire me just because you want to sleep with me. You know that, right? There were ten other companies at the event." I press my hand over her mouth and drag her over the sofa where I sit down and drag her over my lap with her ass up in the air.

I pull down her shorts and panties. "What are you doing?"

"You have several spankings coming, ma belle, but this one is because you doubt your talent and me." My hand comes down on her pretty pale bottom, turning it pink. Marilyn's gasps make me spank her ass cheek again. "Have you learned anything, Marilyn?"

"Nope," she says, lips popping on the "p" sound.

"Bad girl," I growl, spanking her three more times. "I believe you've learned something. You've learned you like your ass spanked." I press my fingers into her tight hole, and it's soaking wet.

"Mr. Beaumont, I hope this isn't the treatment you give all your bad employees."

"Only you. You need to be taught inside and out of the bakery how to behave. After all, we are going to create a family full of little bakers for generations to come."

"Babies?"

"Yes, Marilyn. Did you think I'd just fill anyone with my cream? It's only for you. I want my little ones inside of you." She flexes around my fingers, squeezing them fiercely.

"Fill me up, Julien."

"Avec plaisir, with pleasure," I growl as I fist her hair in my hand, dragging her head up to my face. Her pretty brown eyes are glossy with heated lust. "You're mine, my beautiful Marilyn. God, your ass is so sexy." I rub her ass cheeks. "Do you know how badly I want to fuck this little gushing hole? It's so creamy and wet, waiting for me to put my big dick deep inside and breed you."

I lift her off my knees, raising her ass up to my face so I can lick her slit, loving the taste of her sopping wet cunt. "Give me your cum, baby. Soak my face before I drill you into this sofa because I'm going to fuck you right here and then on your bed."

"We'll see if you're up to it."

I swat her ass hard. "We will see because if my dick isn't hard, you'll be working that jaw good as you blow me, making me ready to take you again, won't you? Because you want to be the best employee, don't you?"

"Yes, I do."

"I can see you do. This pussy is dripping for me. Wet and ready. Come on my tongue and then I'll fuck your pretty little hole."

"Yes, boss."

"Good. I like that." I eat her up sloppily until she comes all over my face and then I drop my slacks, freeing my cock that's ready to unload with just a few strokes for sure. I quickly remove my shirt so I'm completely naked. Then I bend her over the cushions and stand with one knee on the seat and the other foot on the floor, guiding my length inside. The tightness is still so intense that some of my cum shoots out before I move.

I'm still granite hard and I start to fuck her without abandon. My hands grip her waist, one on each side as she holds onto the arm of the sofa for support and then I let loose, slamming in and out. "You feel incredible. I'm about to come in your pussy. Are you ready to come again?"

"Not yet, but I'm close."

"What did I tell you about taking orders?"

"You didn't tell me to come, Mr. Beaumont."

I reach around and pinch her hard nipples and

then grip her face. "I think you like being a very bad employee," I growl against her throat.

"I want to be good," she moans, clenching her walls around my length. It feels too damn good, but the sight of her getting worked up is even better.

"What can I do to make you a better employee?"

"You can kiss me."

"Yes, I can." I tilt her head and crush my mouth to hers, sliding my tongue inside, twisting and playing around with hers and then I pull my lips away and suck on her throat and back to her mouth.

"I'm coming."

"Good because I'm coming too." I unload as she does, coming deep inside her, spraying her walls and filling her with my seed, hoping it takes root because I'm serious about the babies. The rest is dirty talk, but the baby talk is real. She's mine, and I want our family to begin.

We fall onto the sofa and I spoon her little body, cradling her close with my dick still inside. "Are you ready to move this to the bed?"

"When you are," she mumbles sleepily.

I carry her to the bedroom and then take a shower. As much as I'm still turned on and ready to go, I tore apart her business and wore her out. When she's ready, I'll take her again as promised.

In the middle of the night, I wake to her mouth on my cock. "Hey, baby, what are you doing?"

"Just following orders."

"Well, don't let me stop you," I grunt.

One hell of a wake-up call.

Who needs sleep anyway?

Seven

MARILYN

Julien's driver, John, dropped off a fresh set of clothes for him in the morning and then waited for us as we prepared for the day.

It's fall in Chicago, so it's a bit of a mixed bag of weather. One day it's eighty, and then the next day it's forty degrees. Right now, it's a cool fifty-two and breezy so I need a hat and light jacket. When I dig them out of my front closet, I get a growl from Julien. "What? You don't like them?"

"Could you look sexier? It's as if you were meant to sell the outerwear. Come now before I strip you bare and fuck you again."

"You keep that thing in check." I point straight to

that massive cock that's barely hidden by his coat. He smirks, stalking closer, like a wicked villain with dirty intent. "You must behave, Mr. Beaumont. You are my boss and need to keep your hands to yourself."

"I just want one kiss," he says so innocently but those eyes of his are filled with villainous sin.

"Just one." I lift my index finger, and he nods in agreement.

"Okay," I surrender so effortlessly.

His hands slide around me, and I melt into his arms as his mouth lands on me. Three minutes later, he pulls back from the most intense and passionate kiss. I shake myself out of the dazed state he put me in. "I should have known better."

"Come. We're going to be late." He takes my hand and rushes us out of the apartment as if I'm the reason we're behind. I just giggle and deal with his level of intensity.

We pull up to the bakery early in the morning to start going over the plans for the wedding in Paris and handle the daily baked goods for the bakery itself. I'm so excited to be a part of everything. I find Julien staring at me as the vehicle comes to a stop. "What?" I ask.

"Nothing. You're just so damn beautiful when you're happy." I didn't know my joy was so obvious.

I can't hide the blush on my face or the clenching of my thighs at his praise. Am I that easy when it comes to him? "Thank you. I'm excited to get started."

"That's good, because I can't wait for everyone to get a taste of your baked treats." He assists me out of the vehicle and then holds the door open to the bakery. Once inside, I breathe in the delicious smells permeating the air, tasting them on my tongue.

"Mr. Beaumont, Ms. Shaw, good morning." The woman at front of the bakery greets us with such enthusiasm I can't help getting a tad bit jealous. She's a petite blonde who's absolutely breathtakingly beautiful.

"Good morning, Sara. We're heading into the kitchen to start baking. Has Myla arrived already?" Although she could be another man for as much attention Julien showed her.

"Yes, she arrived ten minutes ago," she says with a bright smile.

"Fantastic. And Oliver?" There goes the sunshine in her face. That's a bit strange.

"Sir, he called in." She appears nervous after admitting that, and that explains her crestfallen expression.

"Did he say why?" Julien bites, tension visible in his broad shoulders.

"Only that he wasn't feeling well." Something isn't adding up, and Julien has a weird expression on his face like he's not quite sure what to make of it.

The second we step into the back, I ask, "Are you okay?"

"Yes. I'm fine. I need to make a call after we get settled." He kisses my cheek, and I smile.

"Maybe we shouldn't be kissing at work," I say, knowing how it will look to anyone that sees us.

"Woman, I will kiss you wherever I want. You're mine, even if you work for me. I don't have a policy about it, and I don't give two fucks what anyone has to say about it. Let someone doubt your talents. Once they taste your pastries, they'll bite their tongues."

I lift my purse off my shoulder and then slip off my coat. A low growl comes from Julien as he takes in my top. "Damn, you're so fucking sexy. I don't know how I'm going to make it through the day without bending you over the counter and burying my cock deep inside you."

"Well, we do have an audience, and the fact that it's not quite up to code if we fuck with food around," I remind him.

"I'd hate to waste good desserts, but some things

are just worth it," he grunts, slamming his mouth to mine.

We finally pull apart and then set our things in his office before going into the kitchen area where Myla is working with Thomas, who I haven't met yet, but Julien makes the introductions.

"Myla, I haven't seen you since… what… last September?" I say, walking up to her and giving her a big hug.

She pulls back and smiles. "Yes. It's been so crazy with classes that I didn't have time to work in the test kitchens after hours." She has a family to take care of, and it's sweet how loving her husband is. He supports her career to the fullest.

"I'm sorry. Well, at least you're here, working for Mr. Beaumont."

Julien leans in and whispers in my ear, "Good, ma marguerite, you only get away with calling me Julien."

We get underway and jot down the list of ingredients and supplies. We are planning not only for the storefront to be sold, but the items that are needed just for the wedding event. It takes most of the day and Myla and I are super tired.

Thomas had already left two hours earlier since he started three hours before all of us. He opens early for the morning rush, and then Sara comes in before Julien. They have four other staff members, but those two are Julien's favorites because they are amazing. Thomas is his head assistant baker. Sara runs the front end as the cashier and customer service rep, taking all the special orders.

"Let's call it a night. Tomorrow we'll get started on the cake for the actual wedding. We need to have a backup cake should something happen to the first, so we need a lot of baking and storing. We are going to be put to the test. Let me walk Mrs. Reed to her car first, and then we'll clean up."

"I left my purse and coat in your office, Mr. Beaumont," Myla says.

"We'll gather it first."

He walks her out and then returns a minute later.

"You don't have to do all that by yourself, my sweet morsel. I can help." He moves to stand behind me.

"There's not a lot left to clean. Myla has a knack for keeping an organized workstation. I believe that has a lot to do with being a mother." He unties my apron, letting it fall to the floor in front of me.

"Yes, something I plan to help you with," he growls, gripping my hips and grinding his cock against my ass. I shiver and rub my butt back against his thickness, enjoying the pressure.

"Yes, I believe you suggested that recipe earlier," I answer through a moan as his teeth bite down on my shoulder.

"I've spent all day watching you bake. Have you any idea how erotic that is to me? I nearly came twice like a fucking schoolboy when you licked your lips after testing the icing. Look what we have here." He reaches over, and there's still a bowl of filling.

I slip my finger into the almost empty bowl and lick it off, sucking it for good measure. A low rumble comes from his chest, and I can feel it against my back. He swats my bottom. "You're trying to get fucked rough right here, aren't you?"

"Yes, Mr. Beaumont." He's not the only one who got worked up while baking. The man is an artist in the kitchen.

He quickly yanks down my yoga pants and sees I'm not wearing any panties. His first two fingers immediately push into my pussy hole. I gasp and then moan while he roughly finger fucks my slit.

"Such a bad employee, Ms. Shaw. No panties." He sucks on my throat and then pulls back hard. He goes to his belt and frees his cock from his pants. "Knees, now. You're going to be punished. Do you like cream? I've got some for you." He pushes me down onto the ground and opens my mouth, reaching for the bowl with the other hand and slipping two fingers in and swiping it over his cock.

"Clean me off, woman." Gripping my hair, he guides me to his thick cock and I lick off the first bit of frosting before taking his head into my mouth.

I moan and then begin sucking on his massive thickness. I don't need any icing to take his cock. This man has made me a cock whore. I could gag on it all day if he let me. I don't know what it does to me, but my pussy gushes as I take him deeper and deeper down my throat. Inch by inch, I take him until my nose is buried in his groin. "Good girl."

"Fuck, I'm coming." I reach between my legs and cry out, rubbing my pussy, crying his name. "Julien."

He lifts me up off the floor. "Fuck, you're a dirty girl, aren't you? You're coming from sucking my cock. I haven't even come yet. I guess I'm saving this load for your creamy cunt where it belongs, but first I want to taste that juicy slit." Another swipe of the last of the icing, and the cool frosting hits my clit.

"Fuck," I moan. I'm so sensitive, and then his tongue hits my core. I damn near buck off the table, but he pins my hips down.

"Stay put. I'd hate to write you up for not

following orders. Insubordination will not be tolerated." He slaps my thigh.

"Fuck, what's the punishment, Mr. Beaumont?" He pumps his finger in my pussy a couple of times and then slides it to my rear and then with a pop, pushes just inside my ass.

"Oh," I cry, thighs shaking. It doesn't hurt because I'm soaked and he's not far in, but I'm so turned on that I want him to fuck me hard like a dirty bitch.

"Are you going to take orders?"

"I don't know."

"Well, it doesn't matter because I'll be fucking that little asshole one day. I want to possess every inch of you, Marilyn. I want you to belong to me in every way. Bred in every hole, full of my seed so there isn't a spot I haven't claimed. Do you understand?"

"Yes, Julien. Eat me, fuck me, come inside me, please." I'm practically shouting my needs.

"That's such a good girl."

He sucks on my pussy until I scream his name, and then he stands and readies himself at my entrance. With a smirk, he shoves his cock deep inside with one full thrust. I cry out as the table rocks. My knees are bent to my shoulders as he fucks me hard.

"You're mine, ma marguerite," he grunts. "Say it. Tell me who you belong to."

"You, Julien."

"Fuck, I'm coming," he roars, shooting his load deep into my womb.

He releases my legs and rests his arms on the table, keeping most of his weight off me. "You belong to me too, right?" I ask, feeling a bit insecure. He's so good at fucking me and always demanding my possession, but do I have his?

He looks into my eyes, and there's a tenderness that I've seen several times now since we've met. "Of course. Only you. Only ever you, ma belle." His mouth comes down on mine, pushing him so deep. He pulls back and out of me. His cock is still hard.

"Let's get dressed and finish cleaning up so this place can pass an inspection. I'd hate to get you in trouble," I say.

He's fixing his clothes, picking up his belt off the floor and answers, "It's okay. It will be cleaned easily." He says it like he's done this before, and my inexperience and jealousy slam deep into my heart.

"Is this a regular thing for you?" I ask as I try to fix my messed-up hair. Thankfully I'm fully dressed before I let that slip out. I'm ready to run because my heart's too fragile for the answer.

He whips his head around violently, and he's on me in a second. His hand is in my hair, fisting it as he tugs it back so I can look him in the eyes.

"When I say only, I mean only, Marilyn. I'm a decade older than you, but I lost trust in humanity a long time ago. Then you came along, and I forgot all the distrust because I knew you were my other half. My brother even teased me about it. There is no one else."

"But you're so… powerful and dominant."

He chuckles softly. "Sorry, and thanks, baby. When I'm with you, the boss in me comes out and I want to dominate you. If that means that I appear experienced, I'm sorry, but I'm not, baby girl. You're the only woman I've fucked, and the only one I ever will. Now, let's clean up because I'm not even remotely close to done fucking that hot, sticky cunt tonight. I'm still horny, and I've got a pent-up lust to get out of me."

We've just finished the last of the mopping and sterilization of everything. "I think I'm going to order a new table and move this into my condo."

"Why?"

"Because this is too precious to me. I've fucked

you on this, and I don't want others using it." I can read the seriousness in his words. He means every bit of it.

"Um, if you get a new one, I'm sure you'll fuck me on it too if I stay."

He stalks closer to me, tilting his head while looking at me fiercely. "If you stay?"

"I mean…" His mouth is on me, kissing me hard. I moan, thrusting my hands into his hair and then he presses my ass against the table.

"You're not going anywhere," he grunts against my mouth.

"Um… Mr. Beaumont," I moan just as the kitchen door swings open.

I quickly push him off me to find Sara standing there with her mouth gaping. Her body is quickly slammed against the wall, while a reporter with a camera and the dean of my culinary school are marching in and invading our space.

They rush toward us like they have the right to be in here and I'm mortified.

"Do you seduce all your employees? Is this how you graduated with perfect marks, Ms. Shaw?" the reporter asks while his camera guy points his camera all in my face.

"None of you have a reason to be back here. Get

the fuck out." Julien pulls me behind him. "Mon amour, go into my office."

I follow his orders because I'm beyond uncomfortable being there. Tears fall down my face as I wonder about how much they saw or heard.

"Sara, are you well?" I hear George say as I move toward Julien's office. Where did Julien's brother come from? Why is Sara still here? I open the door and hide inside, feeling the embarrassment set in immediately.

A minute later, the door flies open, and Julien comes rushing in. I can't hide the tears in my eyes. "Maybe it's best that I go."

"The fuck it is. Nothing changes, Marilyn. Nothing. I made that damn clear from the start." He pulls me into his arms and I know that it's the only place I want to be.

Eight

JULIEN

There's a knock on my office door and I want to slam someone's head in until I hear, "Julien, it's me." It's my brother. Releasing my woman, I unlocked the door and open it for George.

"I need you to take Marilyn to the condo, please."

"What? I can go to my place," she says. Yeah fucking right. I'm not ready to ever let her leave my side again, especially after this bullshit.

"No. You will go to the condo and wait for me. I don't know how long this bullshit will take, but for right now, I want to know you're safe. Please do what I tell you."

"Okay."

"Good." My mouth is on hers, kissing my woman softly. "Rest, I'll be there as soon as I can." I trust my brother more than anyone in the world to look after my future wife.

As soon as I walk them out through the back entrance, I head to the front to deal with the assholes who came barging through my property and my employee who let them in.

Heads are going to roll.

"Now, before you open your mouths, I'm going to say that you're only going to get one chance to make your case for why I shouldn't have you arrested for trespassing if not breaking and entering. Ms. Shaw might be my employee, but she's more than that and if I see any store about this, I'll have your asses. Anything to say?"

They begin to explain babbling at first, talking over each other. "Shut up, you. Dean, you go first."

"I was contacted by the reporter about Ms. Shaw the bake-off being a front for selling women in prostitution. I told him it was a lie and he said that he'd gotten a lead from about Ms. Shaw. I came to prove him wrong."

"I was told that Ms. Shaw was going to set you up to be trapped for sexual harassment."

"All of that is a crock of shit."

"Sara, do you care to tell me why you would do this to me?"

She's sobbing and manages to get out between hyperventilating breaths that she had received a text message to return to the office and unlock the shop and give a tour to the dean, by Oliver, no less. She apologized to us, but it's not her I'm pissed at. She's not the one who did this.

Of course, I knew it was all bullshit and set up as a hit piece on me.

I contact the police and file a report. I spend the evening at the bakery with a detective while George tells me that Marilyn is secure in the condo.

It's nearly one in the morning, and I'm beat. We have to be back at the bakery to get the day started in a few hours, so when I get in, Marilyn lets me hold her without a word. I cradle her in my arms and whisper my love even though I know it's too soon for her. "Je t'aime."

"I can't believe we've only got a week until the wedding," Myla says as she slips on her coat. It's been one long day, but I'm ready to get my woman home and naked.

"I know. It's insane," Marilyn adds. "We have been working so hard to make all of these pieces, and they're going to be fabulous."

"The cake is the grand masterpiece, ma marguerite," I say, loving the work she's been doing on the bottom layer. We're setting the layers one by one. Once we land and they set, we'll stack them, but not a moment before.

"What does that mean?" Myla asks.

"Ma marguerite?" Mya nods. "It means my daisy."

"Why do you call her that?"

"Well, the first picture I saw of Marilyn, she was standing next to her daisy cake." Marilyn blushes, knowing that it was her daisy panties that inspired that little pet name for me.

"It's so cute."

"Your hubby doesn't even call you Myla. He just calls you My-love. I think that's perfect."

"It is. He's a good man," I say, having met the man who practically snarls when anyone looks at her. She doesn't know it, but he watches her like a hawk. I don't blame the guy. If Marilyn was out of my sight, I'd feel the same way, but we get to be together all day, every day now.

"He is. I think I'll keep him."

"That's good because I wasn't going to let you leave anyway, baby girl." A growl comes from the front door.

"These men have no damn respect for the laws."

"None."

"As long as you understand that, we're good," I loudly whisper to Marilyn. "Now it's time to go home because I have to put something in the oven."

"The man has the right idea. I'll be the baker tonight, woman." He grabs Myla and carries her out of the bakery.

Sara sighs behind us.

"Are you done? We can give you a ride home," Marilyn offers. Sara is just eighteen and goes to an online community college. She takes the bus to work all the time. I've offered to get her a company car at the very least when I realized it. I know what it's like to be in her shoes and it fucking sucks, but she's extremely embarrassed to take handouts.

"I've got her." George pops through the front door.

"Thanks, but no thanks. I can take the bus." There's a tension between them that concerns me. My brother wouldn't do anything to hurt her, but she is my employee. I move to step in, but Marilyn grabs my hand. "Let's just leave that alone." I look down at my woman, raising my brow.

"Leave it," she insists, dragging me from the bakery.

"What's going on?"

Marilyn and Sara talk while loading the display cases and when they get some free moments. "Let's just say your brother's an ass, and I'm not sure we want to see the fireworks go off."

"Oh shit. Okay." I smirk as we slide into the back of the SUV. I had a feeling he liked her, but she was too young about six months ago.

"I'm ready for a bath and to hit the hay."

"I'm starting to believe that's how you stay so slender. When is the last time you've had a real meal, Marilyn?"

"I believe you are the reason I haven't had much of an appetite for anything but dick and sleep."

"Okay, I suppose you have a point. So no dick until you've had a good night's rest and a hearty meal."

"Sounds good." We pull up to my condo, and there's at least two reporters out there because I happen to live near a fucking celebrity who gets enough attention for the both of us, although he hates it more than I do.

"Chef Beaumont, isn't this your lovely new pastry assistant?" I wonder if someone sent them here even though I threatened to sue the dean and the other reporters. I suppose it could have spread another way. Oliver had been arrested and released, but I have other people who hate me in the industry.

"She's soon to be my wife, but I'll have you know she's the best baker in this duo for sure. Everyone at the baking competition wanted to hire her, and I snagged her first. I assure you, hands down she beats me."

"So was it love at first sight?"

"For me, it certainly was. We met the day before the bake-off. I was supposed to be reviewing the candidates' credentials when I ran into Miss Shaw. One look, and I fell madly in love and had no idea that she was a baker. All I knew was I couldn't let her get away, and I hadn't bothered to open a single file."

"Is that true, Miss Shaw?"

"Yes, I tried to cut and run, but he caught me and now I'm hooked." She smiles with all her heart, and I can't fight the true happiness in my own heart. Let those assholes say anything. Our feelings are there for everyone to see. All the bullshit they can make up is just lies, and the truth is crystal clear.

The two reporters laugh.

"Now, if you'll excuse us. It's been a very long day and we're preparing for a wedding… we're catering for, and we must be getting some rest." I lead her past them and into the building off to the bank of elevators.

"Thanks for grabbing their attention," the handsome bastard says next to me.

I growl a little louder than I planned. I didn't know I could do that involuntarily, but apparently you can when someone with enough testosterone comes near your female. It must be some Animal Planet type shit. "No problem," I grumble.

"What's wrong? I thought I did a good job out there," Marilyn asks.

"You did, doll. He's snarling at me." He has the nerve to wink at my woman.

"Why?"

"Because I'm a hot new actor, and you're beautiful. He doesn't want to lose you to me." Does he not know how to turn off the charm? I'm about to deck his ass and give the reporters a new damn story on how I broke my hand on his chiseled pretty face.

"Well, it ain't gonna happen, anyway."

He throws his hands up. "No offense to either of you, but I wasn't interested, anyway. I was just explaining his caveman behavior. If I ever get a girl I want like that, I wonder if I will stop using more than one syllable at a time? Who knows. Well, this is me. Have fun." He waves us off. Marilyn turns to me and giggles.

"You think it's funny."

"Only a little bit because he's right. I've never heard something so caveman-like before, and I have to say I find it super freaking sexy.

"Then let me make sure we're not using syllables all fucking night, baby."

I carry her out of the elevator and into my condo without letting her feet hit the ground because I need her in bed, taking my dick nice and deep to remind her that I'm her man and no sexy fucker can come between us.

I've officially lost it, and somehow I don't give a rat's ass about it. I tear off her clothes and mine as well. "I need to shower," she says, but I'm not listening because I want that pussy on my mouth. I know that it's all hot and warm, like a sweet apple pie. I bend her over the bed, spreading her legs and lifting her onto her knees.

I dip my tongue along her seam from behind. A growl comes from my throat as I lick the sweet, salty tang off her cunt. I want more. I drive my tongue as deep as it will go, hoping to pull out as much as I can.

She squirms on the bed, getting closer and closer to coming, but she's pulling her sopping wet slit away from my face and I just can't have that. With a grunt, I grab her and flip her onto her back and slide her to the middle of the bed. Parting her legs, I wrap her knees around my elbows and I dive back into her pussy. I feast on her until she's creaming all over my face.

Lifting up onto the mattress, I press my knees onto the bed and then push the head of my cock into her tight little hole. We fuck hard and fast until I have her screaming my name and only my name and then I let go, coming in long streams of cum, letting all of my possessive urges out.

We fall into a heap and let a much-needed sleep come.

Morning comes, and I make sure her breakfast is an all-star one with sausage, bacon, eggs, hashbrowns, and pancakes so she's full. Then, I promise to give her a healthy dicking for lunch, which I do in my office so she's stuffed.

It's near the end of the day when my phone rings, and I take the call in my office while Marilyn bakes in the kitchen.

"Hello, Jack."

"I saw you two on TV."

"Yeah."

"She won't talk to me."

"Honestly, she hasn't really spoken to anyone. We've been busy, but she misses you. If you love her, I will say this." I go on to explain my plan to him and then end the call just as Marilyn knocks on my office door.

"Come in," I call out. "Love, you don't have to knock." I stand up and walk around to greet her with a light kiss to her lips.

"It's your office."

"Consider it yours, too."

"No."

"Anyway. We have a problem. Myla's husband's here, and we need you in the kitchen."

"Okay. I'm coming." I wink at her, and she gives me her usual response to my perverted innuendos: an eye roll.

"So what is the problem?"

"The designs for the wedding have been shared online," he says. He watches his wife like a hawk, so he must know something I don't.

"What? That's not possible."

"It is." She pulls a camera out of the bench table near the door. We look at each other, and she shakes her head.

"It's off now, but it was working for the past week. It turned on when they were here with those reporters. Those weren't reporters. They were here to steal recipes and ideas from us," Marilyn sobs. "The wedding is next week."

"Calm down, mon amour. I'll fix it."

"How did you find this?"

"My husband stalks me… apparently. He found my likeness online and was pissed when I had no idea."

"We'll destroy them."

"Good. I want them ruined. I'll make this better. I have to call Elsa, okay? It might not be a big deal because the bride is a diva. She might want to be the talk of the town."

"Sounds like a good thing, yes, unless it's in a negative light."

"We'll work it out. I promise." I kiss her lips and then head into my office to deal with the wedding planner and her entitled bride who makes every bridezilla look like a sweet sugarplum fairy.

Nine

MARILYN

The flight to Paris is calm and quiet as we go over the plans for the wedding, which have been a freaking mess. We haven't spoken about the supposed impromptu proposal or wedding that was thrown about like it was no big deal the other night in front of the reporters, but it hasn't left my mind for one single minute. Maybe it's because I'm a woman or because I'm madly in love with the man, but it flooded my brain.

Our relationship is new and these feelings are completely irrational, yet I can't chase them away.

Still, I have a job to do, and that's to get this wedding tasting the best and to deliver a cake the bride will be pleased with. Especially after my old dean managed to try and steal my ideas. We had to create new designs for the cake and desserts, working overtime while Myla's husband went hardcore to work refitting the kitchen with enhanced security.

We worked to the bone in the condo, the bakery, and in my apartment. Hell, we didn't even have time to fuck like bunnies over the past week. Which is probably why I'm more unsure of us. It was my dean who violated Julien's personal space, only to have the same thing happen to him again. Maybe he's thought twice about us.

"What's wrong, Marilyn? You've been quiet since we arrived. I thought you would be excited to be here."

"I am." Damn it, that didn't sound convincing at all.

"I don't believe a word you're saying."

"Chef Beaumont," a woman calls out, and she's a perfect beauty, instantly making me jealous. Another reason that maybe we should keep this thing as a fling. Only there's just one problem, or maybe more than one. I don't know if I could live without him now.

I drop my head and walk on, pretending that I don't see them talking, but then Julien reaches out and grabs me. "Where the hell do you think you're going?" he growls in my ear. It sends a sensual chill down my spine and I can't fight the lust that owns me when he does things like that. Julien turns to the woman and says, "Sorry, my fiancée is having a bit of jet lag."

"No problem. That's what happened to me when I got roped into this event. It's almost over, though. I'm the event planner, by the way." She sticks her hand out for me to shake. I do, and she didn't seem to be overtly flirtatious with Julien. In fact, Elsa's nothing but professional, and he doesn't act like she's any different than anyone else.

I meet her and realize that she's not a threat, but there will be plenty of other women that will fall at Julien's feet. He excuses us and leads us up to the hotel room where he takes my hand and pulls me into his arms. Gripping both sides of my face, he pleads, "Please tell me what's wrong with you."

"I don't know what's going on with us," I state.

"What do you mean, what's going on with us?" He backs away, looking at me like he's confused.

"Never mind. I'm just being foolish. I'm in the city of love, and I guess that newspaper article and online post about our relationship has me on edge. I guess your comments were just to shut them up, weren't they?" The words sound even more pathetic when I say them out loud.

We haven't known each other long enough to be talking about marriage and babies and yet here we are, and I feel overwhelmed by the need to make it a reality. Have I lost it and become an insane woman, attaching herself to the first man she sleeps with?

He paces, thrusting his hands in his hair. Finally stopping in front of me, he says, "Woman, we have a job to do." He brushes right past me and out of the hotel room. I follow right behind him and remember that we came here to bake for a wedding, not anything else.

"Of course, you're right, Mr. Beaumont. Let's get to work," I reply, stepping into the elevator without looking at him. I'm not mad at him, just at myself.

"Cher, please."

"No. Whatever is between us can wait. We have to show off our talents in the kitchen." He takes my hand and brings it to his lips, but I pull it away quickly after he kisses the back of my hand. "We should remain professional."

He gazes into my eyes, and I see that he's wounded by my overreaction but I can't take it back. "Very well." We step off the elevator and walk side by side without touching.

For the rest of the day, I keep my distance from him. I can't be around him because my heart is breaking into pieces every time I get the cold shoulder. This past week has been a test of how things get when work is tough, and apparently he pulls away and doesn't want me anymore.

I call the girls, needing someone to talk to, but neither of them answer. Hell, I even call Petra because I'm desperate, but she doesn't answer and I wonder if the damn time zone has something to do with it.

By the end of the night, I fall into a fitful sleep and Julien is nowhere to be found. I wake up in the middle of the night to his arms around me. "I love you, ma marguerite. Je t'aime, Marilyn." Sleep comes to me easily.

JULIEN

I want to surprise her, but she's making it very difficult. Of course it wasn't a fucking way to shut the press up. I have the ring in my pocket this very second and I'd marry her in a heartbeat, but I'm waiting for that asshole brother of hers to arrive with the wedding gown.

It's been a hard thing to pull off via email and text with the occasional phone call when I know she's just in the other room, or hell, even sitting next to me on the plane, but I have every intention of making her my wife.

We've only known each other a short time, but she's my soul mate. I've never met a woman who could capture my heart or even attention. I get that she's pissed at me, but I can't do anything about it without spoiling the surprise. This woman has my heart and will be my wife before we leave Paris.

Tomorrow was the wedding for Alexa and Philippe, who met on a cruise for singles after both having failing marriages. When I arrived, my buddy called me to inform me that the wedding had been called off because Philippe had found her in bed with the best man.

So I made a quick change of plans. Instead of having the wedding the day after theirs, we'd have theirs with the special creations Marilyn and I had created at the last minute. Our family and friends were already on their way, so it was perfect. My friend let me have the venue and everything in exchange for the fees he would have paid for the cake and desserts, so it worked out.

We work for hours and I steal glances at Marilyn, itching to reach over and touch her, to apologize for not telling her that she's the most precious thing in the world to me and that tonight I'd be asking her to marry me.

Her brother has just landed along with my brother and all her friends. Our guest list is massive for an impromptu wedding, but it's fucking great. Everything has to be perfect, but there's one problem. My woman, the love of my life is so damn angry with me.

"We're done. Time to shower and prepare for dinner," I inform her.

"I'm not hungry," she huffs.

"Did I just give a fucking order, Miss Shaw?"

She scrunches up her face dismissively, crossing her arms. "And? I'm off the clock, Mr. Beaumont."

"Enough." I flip her over my shoulder and press the elevator button. I swat her ass twice.

"Hey, jerk. I quit." She covers her ass.

I let out a hard, brief chuckle. "Nope. Not allowed."

"I don't care."

"Didn't you say we don't follow laws?"

"I don't care. You're not the boss of me. You're a jerk. I hate you, Julien." I can hear the tears in her throat and that's too fucking much for me to take. I slide her down my body and pin her to the elevator wall.

With my hand on her throat, I correct her. "No,

you don't. You love me and that's why you're mad at me, but I love you so much I can't live without you, Marilyn. Stop crying, or I'm going to give you something to cry about."

"What are you? My daddy?" Gone is the sadness, and I'm met with pure fire in those gorgeous eyes of hers.

With my other hand I cup her pussy. "Is that what you need? I'll take you over my knee and spank your pretty little ass until you listen to Daddy." Her cunt flexes at my words, hungry for some punishment and that's just what she's going to get.

I get her in the penthouse suite and rip her clothes off, lean her over the bed, parting her thighs and bend down to lick her pussy. "Daddy needs your cookie nice and wet so it's soft and ready for me."

"Fuck," she moans.

"Bad girl, watch that mouth of yours." I swatted her ass. "First, I need you to wear something for me."

"Oh, you're getting kinky, Mr. Beaumont."

"What happened to Daddy?" I question, wanting to hear it come from her horny little mouth.

"Do you like it when I call you Daddy?" My dick jerks hard and I'm about to pass out with the need to get inside her before I nut.

"Yes, little girl, because I'm going to breed you

and you're going to make me a daddy over and over again."

"Breed me, Daddy." I slide the ring on her finger.

"After you agree to marry me."

"Yes, yes. Daddy." I yank down my pants and lift off my shirt in a rush, needing to possess her. I slam my cock into her tight hole, fucking her sopping wet cunt hard and fast, pushing her face into the comforters until she muffling out her orgasm.

"That's it, come on my cock. Squeeze all that cream on me so Daddy can come and breed your womb."

I grip her hair and pull her head back roughly and shoot my load into her, pounding my cock between her ass cheeks. Her asshole is next. I'm feeling possessive as I stare at that ring. A new level unlocked when she threatened to leave. I think my heart fucking almost exploded in the elevator. As I pull out of her pussy, I spin her around.

"Clean my cock. I want you to say sorry for telling me you're leaving me."

"You act like that's a punishment, Julien." She has that fucking sass that I love so much.

"Julien?" I ask, tilting my head.

"Daddy."

"When I have you naked, you've just unleashed

your Daddy, baby girl. Now suck my cock. Get me ready for your ass. I'm going to own it before the guests arrive."

"Guests."

"Yes, your guests. Suck Daddy's cock before your bridal party shows up. You're marrying me tomorrow." This isn't how I wanted to spring it on my wife-to-be, but she asked for it.

Eleven

MARILYN

My pussy's on fire as I stroke his cock. Hearing his words only amplifies the arousal in me, like I just didn't come violently. "We're getting married."

"Suck, baby." I do. I slide my tongue over his salty snake, loving the taste of both of us. I need more of it. "Fuck, you're so good at this. I love the way you take me down while wearing my ring. I've held off giving it to you, but then you started acting like a brat, ruining Daddy's surprise."

Fuck, my pussy's fluttering, so I suck harder and pull off because I'm going to come. I lean back and play with my pussy.

He bends down and grabs me by my hair and my waist, lifting me onto the bed, climbing on top of me. "Ready for me to breed this ass?"

"Yes, Daddy. Will you look into my eyes while you do it?"

"Yes, baby. Look at me while I take what's mine." He reaches between us and soaks his cock in my pussy juices and soaks my asshole and then presses the tip into my puckered hole. I gasp and then his mouth lands on mine, kissing me. "Relax, let Daddy take his hole. Come on, I'm almost in." He bends down and sucks on my nipple, biting down before pushing past the ring and he's inside me.

"Yes, Daddy. Fill me up. I'm a dirty girl. I love you."

"I love you too. I live for you. Now, it's time to fill this hole with cream too. Are you ready to be drilled?"

"Yes, please. It hurts so good. Kiss me and fuck me, Daddy."

"Yes, baby. You need to be dominated, don't you?" he asks as he throws my legs over his shoulders, sending his cock deeper in my asshole. His hips piston down over and over.

"Only from you," I grunt, taking the abuse and loving it, pussy getting wetter and wetter. Julien spreads my cunt juices all over his cock as he slides it in and out to give him the lube while his thumb works my clit.

"Good girl." He strums my pussy like a world-class rockstar, and I'm going to come. I scream out, squirting, and feel his balls tighten as he shoots off in my ass.

His cock slides out of my ass before he lets my legs fall onto the bed before wrapping me up in his arms. "I love you so much, Marilyn. I hope I didn't take it too far."

"God, no, Julien. I loved it. In bed, you can be my daddy. It's so sexy." Fuck, we've taken sex to a new level, and I love it. It's kinky and twisted, but I need it. I didn't know I needed to be fucked like that, but I come so easily when he tells me what to do. How it's possible, I don't know because I'm so independent everywhere else.

"Good. I had no idea what that shit meant until you started pouting in the elevator, then I understood Daddy porn."

"Ooh."

"Hey, I was a fucking thirty-two-year-old virgin. Can you blame me for checking out the internet?"

"No, I read books that have all kinds of stuff in it. I assure you there are new fetishes in them, including now Monster love. I don't know what it is, but I'll stick to the vampires and werewolves."

His phone rings next to us. "Shit, okay. We can pick up on your dirty fantasies later, baby, but I think your guests have arrived."

We climb off the bed in a flash, and I rush into the shower.

A minute later, Julien is in the bathroom in his naked glory and then slides into the shower behind me. "They are checking into their rooms and will meet us at dinner in an hour."

"I can't believe it. Who is here?"

"You'll just have to see."

Silently, I'm praying that it's my brother. I miss him terribly, and I want things back to the way they were before. I know he wasn't trying to be a dick and he wants the best for me. "Now, hurry up. I need to wash up. I can't smell like I've been balls deep in you when I see your brother again for the second time."

"My brother," I gasp, unable to fight the smile.

"Yes, baby. I know you want him here." I bite my lip. He grabs it from my teeth. "Enough. He wants to be here too, Marilyn. He loves you so much."

"Thank you." I kiss him and then pull back. I don't have much time to get ready and work on my apology. I'm out of the shower in five minutes after that revelation. I slip on a pretty red and black dress and matching sling-backs. It's a cute outfit for a night out on a date, which I once thought we'd have. Now, it's a pre-wedding dinner.

Julien steps out of the bathroom with just a towel around his waist, revealing his killer upper body, and another running through his tousled medium brown hair that's darker when wet. Fuck, he's so sexy. "Seriously, I'm marrying a goddess. You are a man's dream come true."

"I was thinking you are so unbelievably hot. A woman's dirty dreams. Every wicked TikTok video waiting for a reveal that doesn't happen."

He drops the towel. "Only you get the reveal." He trots over to his suits and then gets ready in front of me as I watch for another minute before getting off my ass. "Lose interest?"

I frown. "Unfortunately, no. I have to finish getting ready."

He arches his eyebrow, raking his gaze up and down my figure like a horny bastard. "I think you're perfect the way you are."

I tap his chest with my hairbrush. "Yes, but I still have to brush my hair, handsome. We all can't towel dry our hair and walk out looking stunning."

"Sorry." He kisses my cheek and then pats my

ass before walking away to sit on the bed and slip on his socks. There's something so domestic about getting ready together that feels natural. I love it. My heart pumps out of my chest thinking about it.

W e arrive downstairs, and the crowd has gathered at the restaurant. I can't believe he did this for me. Standing front and center is Jack, with Petra on his arm. I smile slightly until I see his grow. It's what I've hoped for and my heart melts when his arms open up. I can't stop myself, and I launch into his waiting embrace. "I've missed you, Jackass."

He chuckles, wrapping me up tight. "I've missed you too. I'm so sorry. I'm so sorry. I didn't mean what I said."

"I know. I just…" I sob as we pull apart.

My brother takes my hand and then looks around to find my husband standing behind me. "Can we go talk for a minute?"

"Sure—that room over there," Julien says, pointing to a private room.

"Thanks."

Jack leads us over there before telling Julien to watch over Petra.

He sits me down in a chair. I'm about to say something when he presses his hand down to my mouth and says, "So let me get this out before I forget my train of thought." I nod and he paces once before saying, "That day, it had nothing to do with you. I know you were talented enough, smart enough to kill the competition, get any position you wanted. It was this man I didn't trust. Yes, I trust him now. Hell, I left my wife in his care because I trust him now, but at the time, I didn't know someone could love you the way you needed to be loved."

"It happened for you and Petra."

"Yes, and I knew how I felt. That was different…. Petra was different. Fuck, Marilyn, I wasn't a mind reader. All I knew was that you were drinking and the guy was after you, only to find out he was your new boss. It scared me because what if you used me as an example of love? I was Petra's boss, and I loved her. Maybe you felt this guy was like me."

"So if he playing me, you'd be to blame me for setting the expectation of love."

"Yes," he sighs.

"What changed?" I ask, staring at my big brother who I've never seen looked so humbled before.

"Well, you didn't talk to me, but then I saw the video online and you two had no idea who the other person was. You met by chance, and the love between you looked real. Then he told me about his plan and how he wanted for us to fix our relationship because he knew it was upsetting you."

"I didn't tell him it was."

He smiles and I'm reminded how much he looks like our father. "That's the thing—you didn't have to, sis. He loves you, so he knows."

"I know he loves me." I've finally allowed myself to truly believe Julien loves me the way I'm madly in love with him.

"Good, because I'm hoping to give you away tomorrow, if that's okay."

"I'd love that." I stand up and throw my arms around him for another big hug.

"Are you two almost done in there? Julien's getting a little antsy," Petra says.

We laugh and move toward the door.

"We're coming." We rush back out to the dinner party to see my fiancé pacing until he notices us. Then his eyes meet mine and a smile stretches on his handsome face.

Walking over to us, he shakes my brother's hand

and then takes mine. "It's time for dinner." I sit next to Julien, who can't wait to touch me. As we sit down, he whispers, "Have I told you how much I love you?"

"Not enough," I tease.

"Then I shall always tell you that you're the love of my life. I love you so much and tomorrow cannot come soon enough." He kisses my hand before the servers bring out the dishes.

Dinner is great as we all chat about everything that has happened since we last met. Although, we have to cut it short so my friends and my sister-in-law can help me prepare for tomorrow.

Julien has now been relegated to another suite, and all the women have gathered in our suite.

"Ladies, thank you. I can't believe we're doing this." My heart is so full that I can't even begin to express the elation I feel.

"Your man is insistent, and so is your brother. Between the two of them, we made it happen overnight." Petra says.

"So voila. Please choose whichever one you like best."

One by one they show me an array of five dresses. Each one lovelier than the next and I'm torn between three. Slapping my hands to my cheeks, I shake my head and fight back the tears of joy. "I can't believe it."

"We got them from your brother's contacts, and all in your size to within a quarter inch," Petra says.

"I can't believe he's doing all this for me," I sigh, knowing he went through a lot of trouble to do this even though I wasn't speaking to him.

"Julien loves you," Casey says.

"I meant Jack," I correct her.

"Your brother loves you, too. Besides, this is one simple phone call and delivery. This took an hour or two, and then we return the other ones. Besides, I do remember someone running around on my behalf because he requested it." Yes, the whole winter outerwear. It was so adorable.

"That was nothing."

"Still, we're family. Anyway, pick one. We have a bet going on which one you'll take."

"Oh, goodness." I try on my top three choices and then one stands out to me the best, and I pick it.

"This is it." Every single one of them laughs. "What? Who won?"

"We all did. We said you'd pick this one because it's just so you," Lacey answers.

I laugh because it's true. The gown is completely an Ancient Grecian design that flows straight to my feet with a bust fitted around my bosom and thick cinched straps with a silk cape embroidered with lace daisies.

"It fits you so perfectly. Julien is going to lose it," Petra says, tugging at the bottom of the dress to fix it as I stand in the mirror.

"I hope so," I sigh.

"Of course he is. The man was drooling over your outfit tonight," Lacey says, wagging her brows.

"I can't believe it. We've only just met, and we're getting married in Paris. Wait, can we?" I hadn't thought about the whole legalities of it.

"Yes, they pulled strings and made it a legal American destination wedding." I sigh with relief because from the moment I met Julien he's had a hold over my heart and soul.

"Now let's have some virgin drinks and bullshit some more before bed. We have a big day tomorrow and not a lot of prep time." That's without a doubt an accurate statement.

CHAPTER
Twelve

JULIEN

I take a deep breath as I wait for Marilyn to come down to me.

It's been one thing after another this morning that made it feel like an eternity. My love for her grows by the second, and so does the fear that something could come between us.

Last night I kept my distance because I had to prepare for the wedding, and honestly, so did she. Besides, she had a gaggle of women in our suite so it wasn't like I could sneak in there and risk seeing any of them in any state of undress.

In the meantime a shit storm happened back home, and I was notified about it, but I don't want it to ruin our wedding day, so I have no intention of telling Marilyn just yet. I'll wait until the day is over. Keeping the truth from her it doesn't help my mood.

My brother knows this is weighing on my soul and is doing his best to handle matters while I sit here trying to figure out how to sort out my mixed emotions. I'm going from rage straight to joy and back again every time I consider what's happening back home.

Her little friend with a crush is going to pay big time when I get my hands on the fucker. I can't tell her what he's done because I'm worried that she might back out of the wedding. Not that I'd let that shit happen.

Damon's already been arrested this morning. After speaking with briefly, I promised to contact them to give them a full interview in a few hours after I've already said my vows to my wife.

Still, every minute that passes and the service doesn't happen, the more nervous I get that she'll find out and put a halt to the wedding. I can't be without my beloved.

Mercifully, the large bells begin to toll. On cue, the wedding music begins and my heart settles. The large wooden doors open and Marilyn elegantly marches my way. Steadily with each step, I see her and I can't fight the smile. Her brother holds her firmly on his arm and I start moving in her direction, but my brother grabs my shoulder.

"Hey. Let him do his job. He only has one of her."

I nod, and she giggles. By the time she makes her way to my side, I feel a lot better. She truly looks like a goddess. "Who gives this woman to his man?"

"I do." He acknowledges. Turning to me he says, "Take care of her."

"Always." He slips her hand in mine and I feel at peace. "You are beautiful Marilyn. I am a lucky man," I whisper before the priest begins. Soon we say our vows and slide on our rings.

Looking into her eyes, I let her see the love I have for her as I say it. "I love you, Marilyn Beaumont."

"I love you, my husband."

"Let us welcome Mr. and Mrs. Julien Beaumont."

The guests cheer and clap, blowing bubbles as we exit with pictures going in full force. We head into the reception area, and I'm happy as a can be, but I have a secret that I need to share with my bride. Tension fills my chest.

Jack leans in as Marilyn speaks to one of her friends and he whispers, "Save it for later. Let her have this happy memory."

"I hate having a lie between us," I explained. It's not easy starting off our marriage with such a secret.

"I know, but she'll be crying on her wedding day."

"True." With that, I can calm down. Seeing Marilyn's tears is too much for me to bear.

"Time to twirl your bride around." I do until Jack takes over.

The wedding is almost over, and my wife smiles sweetly as I pull her in for another dance. "You're so lucky that I know that you're trying not to break my heart."

"What? What do you mean?"

"The fire."

"You know?" She knows and she's been this calm all morning?

"Yes. I received a text and then I saw you and Jack talking earlier. You kept it from me so I wouldn't be upset on my wedding day. That's sweet of you, but how are you? How much damage is from the kitchen oven?" she asks.

"Kitchen oven?"

"Yeah, it's only a small fire, right?" That explains her relaxed response. As stressful as a small kitchen fire is, it's like an accident.

"Baby, who sent you the message?" I ask her.

Everyone who had a chance to learn about the bakery knew the truth.

She blushes and ducks her head. "You're going to be mad. I don't know how he even got my number."

I tip her chin to have her look at me. "He?"

"Damon?"

"Damon? The fuck from the bake-off," I growl.

"Yeah, we were classmates, but like I told the girls, he never had my number. My brother made it clear that I didn't give it out to men for a good reason."

I chuckle, knowing this helped add to the case even more. "I love your brother more and more every day."

"What about me?" she challenges, pouting so prettily.

I wrap my arm around her waist and drag her body firmly against mine. "You're my queen, my everything. I live for you." I kiss her hard before pulling back. There are matters that can't wait to be dealt with. "I need to speak with Myla's husband."

"He's over there." She points toward the corner where Jack and Myla's husband are in deep discussion.

"Give me a minute, love. Go sit with Petra, please. I need a word with Jack as well." I start heading toward them when I have a question. "Oh, and when did you receive the message?"

"It came in before I woke up this morning, so I don't know. Here's my phone." I kiss her lips.

"Thanks, love."

The bastard could blow up my bakery, and that's fine because we're here. No one was inside, but that's only because I had it closed down for the impromptu wedding and he had no idea. He thought we'd be inside by the time it went off. I hope they give him attempted murder charges.

I talk to the guys, and it's clear this bastard was hoping she knew about the fire first. He knew she and I were in Paris, but not that all of my staff were going to be here as well.

"We have evidence on top of whatever you can gather from your cameras on that Damon asshole."

"You know he's related to the dean, right? I'm guessing that's how he got her number and why he's so eager for revenge," Myla's husband says.

"I'm betting because he wanted to fuck my wife. I will kill the bastard if I get my hands on him."

"What makes you think that?"

"He told me that when I met the little pencil dick. He was pissed that I swooped in and stole her away before he could keep staying in the friend zone."

"Yeah, Myla never liked that guy. I saw him lurking by them once, and she told me he was interested in Marilyn. I said it was clear she had no intention of giving him more than a pencil to borrow."

"Yeah, well, the asshole will pay big time. Marilyn thinks it's just a small fire."

"She doesn't know there's no fucking building at all? That a couple of windows in other buildings were blown out?"

"Nope. I didn't have the heart to hurt her yet."

"Break it to her now. The night is over," my brother-in-law says.

"Okay. I'm taking my wife to bed." I wink at him, knowing he will think I'm talking about fucking her.

"Wedding night or not, I don't need to hear that. She's still my little sister."

"Well, pervert, I wasn't talking about sex. We've had a very long, busy day and I'm sure your sister isn't feeling too good, especially after the news I'm about to break to her. Goodnight."

I walk over to my wife, and seeing the fatigue in her eyes, I don't bother to ask for permission as I scoop her up into my arms and carry her away. "Say goodnight, Mrs. Beaumont."

"Yes, Daddy," she whispers against my chest.

"Fuck, Marilyn." My dick stiffens in my tux slacks.

"I missed you last night." Her mouth brushes against my throat.

"I missed you too."

"Can we save whatever bad thing you're going to tell me for tomorrow? Let's save tonight."

"Yes, my love." I'll give my wife whatever she wants, including several wedding night orgasms.

Epilogue

MARILYN

"It's coming along nicely. I bet you can't wait to get in there and grab a sweet treat," a stranger says, looking at my rounded belly. I know the second Julien notices he's going to want to jump through the brand-new glass and attack this obvious man.

"Yep," I answer, pressing my lips closed, cheeks puffed out in annoyance. I stare at the sign, liking the look of the new bakery, *La Marguerite*.

Today's the building's final inspection before we can officially open. We've been through a great deal to make it happen in a short time. It takes a lot to bring a business from the ashes and up and running.

This is a new location because we didn't want to

have the memories of the old one in our minds. After they cleared out the rubble, we went to inspect it and the sight of the old one sent me into tears and into the hospital.

That's when we found out that my husband had done what he'd promised. I had a little bun in the oven. It's not so little of a bun now.

At almost nine months pregnant now, I'm due any day, so I didn't want to miss this. I'm not allowed to bake anymore since I can't see the table and my belly is in the way.

At least I can sit, watch, and sample finished products, of course. It happens to be my favorite part of the job. Although my doctor does like me to keep an eye on my sugar intake because gestational diabetes is a real thing.

"Is there something you need?" my security snarls to the man standing way too close to me just as Julien looks up in the window to see the scene before him. His expression changes from a smile to pure anger. Strangely it makes me horny to see.

"I'm actually due inside there. I was only asking a question." Without hesitation, my husband is outside and quickly approaching us.

"I suggest you don't ask her any questions and keep your eyes off her," my husband says.

"Ma marguerite, what are you doing out here in the heat? You should be in bed where I left you," he growls the last part in my ear.

I kiss his lips. "I wanted to be here for the final run-through. The baby is coming soon, and I'm going to miss everything." I pout.

"I'm sorry, my love. Come inside out of the heat." He looks past me. "Who are you?"

"That's the inspector."

"Well, if you want to keep your job, I expect you to inspect the building and not my wife, or your job isn't the only thing you'll be losing." He looked down at the guy's junk. "Do you understand me?"

"Are you threatening a government employee?"

"Is a government employee sexually harassing a client? If you think I missed you staring at my wife's breasts, you are mistaken. I caught it before she did. You only noticed your misstep when I came to greet her. Now, do you understand me or not?"

"I understand."

"Good. Get to it or get out." The warning is all he'll get. He may look civilized, but when it comes to me, he's a different creature altogether.

I love this man. He's intense and insane, but he's right. I try to give men the benefit of the doubt, but my big tits have only grown since I got pregnant and now they're on display all the time, especially when my belly and my tits are fighting for space with my clothes.

"Excuse us," I say, taking Julien's hand and lead him into the shop. "Bruce, take the inspector around please. I need a word with my husband."

Still, I drag my husband to his office and sit on his lap. Running my hands over his chest, his heart slams against my fingers as it beats out of control. "Calm down, Julien. You're too riled up. It's not good to get all worked up for nothing. It's not like he could see down my blouse."

"It's the attempt that matters," he mutters through clenched teeth.

"I know. I'm just trying to make you feel better. Besides, that just means you have a super-hot wife, and it wasn't like you were standing there with me. Now that would be a real insult. I won't always be this good looking." I spear my fingers through his thick hair. My breasts grazing his chin in the process and earning a growl from my always horny husband.

"You'll always be hot to me. I don't give a shit if we're old oatmeal raisin cookies. You'll still be my beautiful cookie."

I let out a barking laugh and manage a quick

"Thank you. Although I could do without the image for now."

"Okay, for now, I need something from you. Before I send your ass back home, lift up your sundress and ride Daddy's cock because he wants to feel his baby girl's warmth at least once more before his little one comes."

"Yes." I straddle him and move my panties to the side as he pulls out his thick length. With his help, I slide down his pole and bounce.

"Sweet, baby girl. You feel so good," he grunts.

"Yes, Daddy. This is what I needed. I'm going to come. Fuck me hard. Spank me." I'm always ready to take him these days.

"That's my baby girl. Let that prick hear you getting drilled. Take that dick deep in your tight, tiny, bred pussy." He fists my hair and then uses his other hand to tug down my sundress and pull out my tit to suck on the tender nipple. I come instantly.

"I'm coming, Daddy. I'm coming on your big cock."

"That's a good girl. Take what Daddy gives you." He thrusts up as I grind my orgasm on his lap until I feel him flood my core with his cum, his face buried in my chest.

With a possessive grunt, he whispers, "Only I get to inspect you."

I grip his hair and drag his face to mine and then ask, "Did I pass your inspection?"

"Yes, but I'll need another inspection later to make sure I'm thorough."

"Of course. I would never expect anything less from you." Giggling, I kiss his chin and then his mouth until I we were both exhausted.

***

The bakery past the inspection of course, unfortunately, though my personal second inspection had to wait another six weeks because I went into labor as soon as we got home. Our son was born two weeks early, but still a healthy nine and a half pounds.

JULIEN

"Congratulations, Marilyn."

"Congratulations, Mommy!" Jules says, calling from his seat. We left the other kids at home because he's the only one who can sit still for more than an hour at a time.

He's six years old and our oldest. With two other little ones, I'm surprised my wife had time to go back to school and get a Special Education Teaching degree.

It all started when Marilyn volunteered to teach a baking class for kids at a local fair one year, and there was a kid there who had autism and it bothered her that the kid had struggled even though she'd been twice the age of the other kids. It broke her heart to pieces, and she ended up giving the girl most of her attention.

My beautiful wife couldn't let that go, having the day stick with her for weeks after the event. She decided there had to be something she could do.

She's already a teaching assistant at a high school, and she's opening her own program in our own building next to our new bakery. Jack and Petra have donated to the special bakery. He's happy to finally give Marilyn the bakery he promised, even if it's not the one he first had in mind.

"There you are, my darling wife. Congratulations are in order, and I believe we are due to celebrate."

"Yes, we are. How about we take this boy home and check on our other little ones?"

"I'm sure they're driving their aunt and uncle nuts."

"I'm so glad Jack is watching them."

"How are you feeling, ma marguerite?"

"I'm well. Why?" I eye her suspiciously, knowing something isn't right.

"You look a little pale." I press my hand to her forehead to make sure she doesn't have a fever. The little one had a fever and a stomach bug last week, and I hoped no one else caught it. Maybe she wasn't lucky after all.

"I'm fine." She playfully swats my hand off her head and takes it in hers.

"Don't lie to me, wife," I warn her.

"I truly am just fine. It's just I think I… well… you've done it again." She grins mischievously and a smile of my own starts involuntarily spreading across my face.

"Oh…" I raise my brows. We don't bother using any protection because I want a dozen little bakers of my own, but her body determines when she is ready. The three boys have been spaced out, so it must mean that she's about to give me another little one. "Are you telling me that I'm going to be a daddy again?"

"You're always my daddy," she whispers.

"Later, you'll be saying that on your knees. We're in a crowd of people and with your son, who is at the height of my waist," I growl as my dick beats against my zipper.

"So spank me," she says in my ear.

"Oh, I will," I whisper. I take my son's hand and lead him out of the masses.

"Daddy, please don't spank Mommy. It's her special day. She's probably too excited to behave."

"I'm only teasing Mommy, son." I look over his head at her and fight back a smile.

We get back home after we drop off Jules with his uncle so I can do some private celebrating with Mommy. First, we check to see if Mommy is indeed giving me another little one.

With a positive test and the all-clear sign that she's feeling better, I send her to her knees to receive her punishment, reward, or whatever she calls it. All I know is that it's fucking bliss to be married to this woman, and I wouldn't have it any other way.

THE END

Find C.M. Steele on:

Website/Newsletter: www.cmsteele.com

Amazon Author Page: www.amazon.com/C-M-Steele/e/B00MQ9FPZS/

Facebook: www.facebook.com/CMsteele2014

TikTok: www.tiktok.com/@authorcmsteele

Instagram: https://www.instagram.com/c.m._steele/

Twitter: https://twitter.com/Author_CMSteele

BookBub: https://www.bookbub.com/authors/c-m-steele

A Best Friends Duet:

Picture Perfect * Instant Obsession

Best Friends Series:

Always You * His Dirty Secret * Sleep Tight

Bianchi Crime Family:

Married to the Mob * Captured by the Mob * Owned by the Mob

Cavanaugh Security Series:

Protecting Macy * Securing Blake

The Cline Brothers of Colorado:

Whatever it Takes * Finding Paradise

Dirty Boss Series:

My Pet * My Cookie * My Flower * My Valentine

The Falling Series:

Falling for the Boss * Falling for the Enemy * Falling Hard

The Fiore Family:

Christmas with the Beast * Christmas with the Boss

Christmas with the Sheriff

Gimme Series:

Sugar * Luck * Rain * Cream * Heat * Love

The James Family:

No Choice * No Way Out * No More Waiting

Keepsakes:

Keeping Blossom * Keep in Mind

The Lamian Wars:

Bound * Reveal * Release

All Hallows Eve

The Middleton Hotels:

Built for Me * Built to Last * Built Strong

Built Over Time * Built Overnight

Nothing but Trouble Series:

Taking the Bait * Taking the Mafia Princess

The O'Connell Family:

Claiming Red * Burning for Claire

Claiming Abby * Reminding Red

Obsessed Alpha Series:

Stone * Cole * Graham

Theo * Maddox *Alessandro

Tony * Cormack * Cameron

Reynolds Ranch Series:

Lara * Tobias

A Rocky Start Series:

Rocky Waters * Her Rock * Rocky Start

A Rough Hands Novella:

My Miracle * Nailing my Wife

Say Something Series:

Say Uncle *Say Please * Say Uncle: Doggy Style

Second Generation:

Say Yes

Sister Switch:

Testing Her Professor * Assisting Her Boss

A Steele Christmas:

Mason's Winter * Perfectly Wrapped * The Company You Keep

A Steele Fairy Tale:

My Gold * My Forever

My Property * My Prince Charming

A Steele Riders Family Novella Series:

Holiday Knockout * His Siren

Steele Riders MC Series:

Boomer * Mick * Jackson * Doc * Beast * Ghost

Wrench * Blade * Boss * Cowboy * Law

<u>Southern Hospitality:</u>

Down South * Gone South

<u>Sweetheart's Treats:</u>

Sweet Surprise * Doctor's Orders, Sweetheart * Sweet Surrender

<u>Twin Sin:</u>

Stalk Me Please * Sinful Intent

<u>White Wolf Ridge Series:</u>

Turner

<u>Wolfe Creek Series:</u>

Wolfe's Den * Beta: Her Alpha

Raging Kane * Written in History

<u>Standalones:</u>

Buying Love * Conquering Alexandria * Ecstasy Captured

Grant's Deal * In Heat * Intense * Killer Abs * Love Discovered

Loving My Neighbor * Mrs. Valentine * My Christmas Gift

Rainy Days * Stormy Nights * Red Hot Nights

Room Service * Scarred * Sharp Curves

So Wrong * Standing There * The Mobster's Virgin

The Wedding Guest * Unexpected